Yet Again

Sir Max Beerbohm

Alpha Editions

This edition published in 2024

ISBN : 9789362992352

Design and Setting By
Alpha Editions
www.alphaedis.com
Email - info@alphaedis.com

As per information held with us this book is in Public Domain.
This book is a reproduction of an important historical work. Alpha Editions uses the best technology to reproduce historical work in the same manner it was first published to preserve its original nature. Any marks or number seen are left intentionally to preserve its true form.

YET AGAIN
BY MAX BEERBOHM

Till I gave myself the task of making a little selection from what I had written since last I formed a book of essays, I had no notion that I had put, as it were, my eggs into so many baskets—The Saturday Review, The New Quarterly, The New Liberal Review, Vanity Fair, The Daily Mail, Literature, The Traveller, The Pall Mall Magazine, The May Book, The Souvenir Book of Charing Cross Hospital Bazaar, The Cornhill Magazine, Harper's Magazine, and The Anglo-Saxon Review...Ouf! But the sigh of relief that I heave at the end of the list is accompanied by a smile of thanks to the various authorities for letting me use here what they were so good as to require.

M. B.

THE FIRE

If I were 'seeing over' a house, and found in every room an iron cage let into the wall, and were told by the caretaker that these cages were for me to keep lions in, I think I should open my eyes rather wide. Yet nothing seems to me more natural than a fire in the grate.

Doubtless, when I began to walk, one of my first excursions was to the fender, that I might gaze more nearly at the live thing roaring and raging behind it; and I dare say I dimly wondered by what blessed dispensation this creature was allowed in a domain so peaceful as my nursery. I do not think I ever needed to be warned against scaling the fender. I knew by instinct that the creature within it was dangerous—fiercer still than the cat which had once strayed into the room and scratched me for my advances. As I grew older, I ceased to wonder at the creature's presence and learned to call it 'the fire,' quite lightly. There are so many queer things in the world that we have no time to go on wondering at the queerness of the things we see habitually. It is not that these things are in themselves less queer than they at first seemed to us. It is that our vision of them has been dimmed. We are lucky when by some chance we see again, for a fleeting moment, this thing or that as we saw it when it first came within our ken. We are in the habit of saying that 'first impressions are best,' and that we must approach every question 'with an open mind'; but we shirk the logical conclusion that we were wiser in our infancy than we are now. 'Make yourself even as a little child' we often say, but recommending the process on moral rather than on intellectual grounds, and inwardly preening ourselves all the while on having 'put away childish things,' as though clarity of vision were not one of them.

I look around the room I am writing in—a pleasant room, and my own, yet how irresponsive, how smug and lifeless! The pattern of the wallpaper blamelessly repeats itself from wainscote to cornice; and the pictures are immobile and changeless within their glazed frames—faint, flat mimicries of life. The chairs and tables are just as their carpenter fashioned them, and stand with stiff obedience just where they have been posted. On one side of the room, encased in coverings of cloth and leather, are myriads of words, which to some people, but not to me, are a fair substitute for human company. All around me, in fact, are the products of modern civilisation. But in the whole room there are but three things living: myself, my dog, and the fire in my grate. And of these lives the third is very much the most intensely vivid. My dog is descended, doubtless, from prehistoric wolves; but you could hardly decipher his pedigree on his mild, domesticated face. My dog is as tame as his master (in whose veins flows the blood of the old cavemen). But time has not tamed fire. Fire is as wild a thing as when Prometheus snatched it from the empyrean. Fire in my grate is as fierce and terrible a thing as when it was lit by my ancestors, night after night, at the mouths of their caves, to scare away the ancestors of my dog. And my dog regards it with the old wonder and misgiving. Even in his sleep he opens ever and again one eye to see that we are in no danger. And the fire glowers and roars through its bars at him with the scorn that a wild beast must needs have for a tame one. 'You are free,' it rages, 'and yet you do not spring at that man's throat and tear him limb from limb and make a meal of him!' and, gazing at me, it licks its red lips; and I, laughing good-humouredly, rise and give the monster a shovelful of its proper food, which it leaps at and noisily devours.

Fire is the only one of the elements that inspires awe. We breathe air, tread earth, bathe in water. Fire alone we approach with deference. And it is the only one of the elements that is always alert, always good to watch. We do not see the air we breathe—except sometimes in London, and who shall say that the sight is pleasant? We do not see the earth revolving; and the trees and other vegetables that are put forth by it come up so slowly that there is no fun in watching them. One is apt to lose patience with the good earth, and to hanker after a sight of those multitudinous fires wherever it is, after all, but a thin and comparatively recent crust. Water, when we get it in the form of a river, is pleasant to watch for a minute or so, after which period the regularity of its movement becomes as tedious as stagnation. It is only a whole seaful of water that can rival fire in variety and in loveliness. But even the spectacle of sea at its very best—say in an Atlantic storm—is less thrilling than the spectacle of one building ablaze. And for the rest, the sea has its hours of dulness and monotony, even when it is not wholly calm. Whereas in the grate even a quite little fire never ceases to be amusing and inspiring until you let it out. As much fire as would correspond with a handful of earth or a tumblerful of water is yet a joy to the eyes, and a lively suggestion of grandeur. The other elements, even as presented in huge samples, impress us as less august than fire. Fire alone, according to the legend, was brought down from Heaven: the rest were here from the dim outset. When we call a thing earthy we impute cloddishness; by 'watery' we imply insipidness; 'airy' is for something trivial. 'Fiery' has always a noble significance. It denotes such things as faith, courage, genius. Earth lies heavy, and air is void, and water flows down; but flames aspire, flying back towards the heaven they came from. They typify for us the spirit of man, as apart from aught that is gross in him. They are the symbol of purity, of triumph over corruption. Water, air, earth, can all harbour corruption; but where flames are, or have been, there is innocence. Our love of fire comes partly, doubtless, from our natural love of destruction for destruction's sake. Fire is savage, and so, even after all these centuries, are we, at heart. Our civilisation is but as the aforesaid crust that encloses the old planetary flames. To destroy is still the strongest instinct of our nature. Nature is still 'red in tooth and claw,' though she has begun to make fine flourishes with tooth-brush and nail-scissors. Even the mild dog on my hearth-rug has been known to behave like a wolf to his own species. Scratch his master and you will find the caveman. But the scratch must be a sharp one: I am thickly veneered. Outwardly, I am as gentle as you, gentle reader. And one reason for our delight in fire is that there is no humbug about flames: they are frankly, primaevally savage. But this is not, I am glad to say, the sole reason. We have a sense of good and evil. I do not pretend that it carries us very far. It is but the tooth-brush and nail-scissors that we flourish. Our innate instincts, not this acquired sense, are what the world really hinges on. But this acquired sense is an integral part of our minds. And we revere fire because we have come to regard it as especially the foe of evil—as a means for destroying weeds, not flowers; a destroyer of wicked cities, not of good ones.

The idea of hell, as inculcated in the books given to me when I was a child, never really frightened me at all. I conceived the possibility of a hell in which were eternal flames to destroy every one who had not been good. But a hell whose flames were eternally impotent to destroy these people, a hell where evil was to go on writhing yet thriving for ever and ever, seemed to me, even at that age, too patently absurd to be appalling. Nor indeed do I think that to the more credulous children in England can the idea of eternal burning have ever been quite so forbidding as their nurses meant it to be. Credulity is but a form of incaution. I, as I have said, never had any wish to play with fire; but most English children are strongly attracted, and are much less afraid of fire than of the dark. Eternal darkness, with a biting east-wind, were to the English fancy a far more fearful prospect than eternal flames. The notion of these flames arose in Italy, where heat is no luxury, and shadows are lurked in, and breezes prayed for. In England the sun, even at its strongest, is a weak vessel. True, we grumble whenever its radiance is a trifle less watery than usual. But that is precisely because we are a people whose nature the sun has not mellowed—a dour people, like all northerners, ever ready to make the worst of things. Inwardly, we love the sun, and long for it to come nearer to us, and to come more often. And it is partly because this craving is unsatisfied that we cower so fondly over our open hearths. Our fires are makeshifts for sunshine. Autumn after autumn, 'we see the swallows gathering in the sky, and in the osier-isle we hear their noise,' and our hearts sink. Happy, selfish little birds, gathering so lightly to fly whither we cannot follow you, will you not, this once, forgo the lands of your desire? 'Shall not the grief of the old time follow?' Do winter with us, this once! We will strew all England, every morning, with bread-crumbs for you, will you but stay and help us to play at summer! But the delicate cruel rogues pay no heed to us, skimming sharplier than ever in pursuit of gnats, as the hour draws near for their long flight over gnatless seas.

Only one swallow have I ever known to relent. It had built its nest under the eaves of a cottage that belonged to a friend of mine, a man who loved birds. He had a power of making birds trust him. They would come at his call, circling round him, perching on his shoulders, eating from his hand. One of the swallows would come too, from his nest under the eaves. As the summer wore on, he grew quite tame. And when summer waned, and the other swallows flew away, this one lingered, day after day, fluttering dubiously over the threshold of the cottage. Presently, as the air grew chilly, he built a new nest for himself, under the mantelpiece in my friend's study. And every morning, so soon as the fire burned brightly, he would flutter down to perch on the fender and bask in the light and warmth of the coals. But after a few weeks he began to ail; possibly because the study was a small one, and he could not get in it the exercise that he needed; more probably because of the draughts. My friend's wife, who was very clever with her needle, made for the swallow a little jacket of red flannel, and sought to divert his mind by teaching him to perform a few simple tricks. For a while he seemed to regain his spirits. But presently he moped more than ever, crouching nearer than ever to the fire, and, sidelong, blinking dim weak reproaches at his disappointed master and mistress. One swallow, as the adage truly says, does not make a summer. So this one's mistress hurriedly made for him a little overcoat of sealskin, wearing which, in a muffled cage, he was personally conducted by his master straight through to Sicily. There he was nursed back to health, and liberated on a sunny plain. He never returned to his English home; but the nest he built under the mantelpiece is still preserved in case he should come at last.

When the sun's rays slant down upon your grate, then the fire blanches and blenches, cowers, crumbles, and collapses. It cannot compete with its archetype. It cannot suffice a sun-steeped swallow, or ripen a plum, or parch the carpet. Yet, in its modest way, it is to your room what the sun is to the world; and where, during the greater part of the year, would you be without it? I do not wonder that the poor, when they have to choose between fuel and food, choose fuel. Food nourishes the body; but fuel, warming the body, warms the soul too. I do not wonder that the hearth has been regarded from time immemorial as the centre, and used as the symbol, of the home. I like the social tradition that we must not poke a fire in a friend's drawing-room unless our friendship dates back full seven years. It rests evidently, this tradition, on the sentiment that a fire is a thing sacred to the members of the household in which it burns. I dare say the fender has a meaning, as well as a use, and is as the rail round an altar. In 'The New Utopia' these hearths will all have been rased, of course, as demoralising relics of an age when people went in for privacy and were not always thinking exclusively about the State. Such heat as may be needed to prevent us from catching colds (whereby our vitality would be lowered, and our usefulness to the State impaired) will be supplied through hot-water pipes (white-enamelled), the supply being strictly regulated from the municipal water-works. Or has Mr. Wells arranged that the sun shall always be shining on us? I have mislaid my copy of the book. Anyhow, fires and hearths will have to go. Let us make the most of them while we may.

Personally, though I appreciate the radiance of a family fire, I give preference to a fire that burns for myself alone. And dearest of all to me is a fire that burns thus in the house of another. I find an inalienable magic in my bedroom fire when I am staying with friends; and it is at bedtime that the spell is strongest. 'Good night,' says my host, shaking my hand warmly on the threshold; you've everything you want?' 'Everything,' I assure him; 'good night.' 'Good night.' 'Good night,' and I close my door, close my eyes, heave a long sigh, open my eyes, set down the candle, draw the armchair close to the fire (my fire), sink down, and am at peace, with nothing to mar my happiness except the feeling that it is too good to be true.

At such moments I never see in my fire any likeness to a wild beast. It roars me as gently as a sucking dove, and is as kind and cordial as my host and hostess and the other people in the house. And yet I do not have to say anything to it, I do not have to make myself agreeable to it. It lavishes its warmth on me, asking nothing in return. For fifteen mortal hours or so, with few and brief intervals, I have been making myself agreeable, saying the right thing, asking the apt question, exhibiting the proper shade of mild or acute surprise, smiling the appropriate smile or laughing just so long and just so loud as the occasion seemed to demand. If I were naturally a brilliant and copious talker, I suppose that to stay in another's house would be no strain on me. I should be able to impose myself on my host and hostess and their guests without any effort, and at the end of the day retire quite unfatigued, pleasantly flushed with the effect of my own magnetism. Alas, there is no question of my imposing myself. I can repay hospitality only by strict attention to the humble, arduous process of making myself agreeable. When I go up to dress for dinner, I have always a strong impulse to go to bed and sleep off my fatigue; and it is only by exerting all my will-power that I can array myself for the final labours: to wit, making myself agreeable to some man or woman for a minute or two before dinner, to two women during dinner, to men after dinner, then again to women in the drawing-room, and then once more to men in the smoking-room. It is a dog's life. But one has to have suffered before one gets the full savour out of joy. And I do not grumble at the price I have to pay for the sensation of basking, at length, in solitude and the glow of my own fireside.

Too tired to undress, too tired to think, I am more than content to watch the noble and ever-changing pageant of the fire. The finest part of this spectacle is surely when the flames sink, and gradually the red-gold caverns are revealed, gorgeous, mysterious, with inmost recesses of white heat. It is often thus that my fire welcomes me when the long day's task is done. After I have gazed long into its depths, I close my eyes to rest them, opening them again, with a start, whenever a coal shifts its place, or some belated little tongue of flame spurts forth with a hiss.... Vaguely I liken myself to the watchman one sees by night in London, wherever a road is up, huddled half-awake in his tiny cabin of wood, with a cresset of live coal before him.... I have come down in the world, and am a night-watchman, and I find the life as pleasant as I had always thought it must be, except when I let the fire out, and awake shivering.... Shivering I awake, in the twilight of dawn. Ashes, white and grey, some rusty cinders, a crag or so of coal, are all that is left over from last night's splendour. Grey is the lawn beneath my window, and little ghosts of rabbits are nibbling and hobbling there. But anon the east will be red, and, ere I wake, the sky will be blue, and the grass quite green again, and my fire will have arisen from its ashes, a cackling and comfortable phoenix.

SEEING PEOPLE OFF

I am not good at it. To do it well seems to me one of the most difficult things in the world, and probably seems so to you, too.

To see a friend off from Waterloo to Vauxhall were easy enough. But we are never called on to perform that small feat. It is only when a friend is going on a longish journey, and will be absent for a longish time, that we turn up at the railway station. The dearer the friend, and the longer the journey, and the longer the likely absence, the earlier do we turn up, and the more lamentably do we fail. Our failure is in exact ratio to the seriousness of the occasion, and to the depth of our feeling.

In a room, or even on a door-step, we can make the farewell quite worthily. We can express in our faces the genuine sorrow we feel. Nor do words fail us. There is no awkwardness, no restraint, on either side. The thread of our intimacy has not been snapped. The leave-taking is an ideal one. Why not, then, leave the leave-taking at that? Always, departing friends implore us not to bother to come to the railway station next morning. Always, we are deaf to these entreaties, knowing them to be not quite sincere. The departing friends would think it very odd of us if we took them at their word. Besides, they really do want to see us again. And that wish is heartily reciprocated. We duly turn up. And then, oh then, what a gulf yawns! We stretch our arms vainly across it. We have utterly lost touch. We have nothing at all to say. We gaze at each other as dumb animals gaze at human beings. We 'make conversation'—and such conversation! We know that these are the friends from whom we parted overnight. They know that we have not altered. Yet, on the surface, everything is different; and the tension is such that we only long for the guard to blow his whistle and put an end to the farce.

On a cold grey morning of last week I duly turned up at Euston, to see off an old friend who was starting for America.

Overnight, we had given him a farewell dinner, in which sadness was well mingled with festivity. Years probably would elapse before his return. Some of us might never see him again. Not ignoring the shadow of the future, we gaily celebrated the past. We were as thankful to have known our guest as we were grieved to lose him; and both these emotions were made evident. It was a perfect farewell.

And now, here we were, stiff and self-conscious on the platform; and, framed in the window of the railway-carriage, was the face of our friend; but it was as the face of a stranger—a stranger anxious to please, an appealing stranger, an awkward stranger. 'Have you got everything?' asked one of us, breaking a silence. 'Yes, everything,' said our friend, with a pleasant nod. 'Everything,' he repeated, with the emphasis of an empty brain. 'You'll be able to lunch on the train,' said I, though this prophecy had already been made more than once. 'Oh yes,' he said with conviction. He added that the train went straight through to Liverpool. This fact seemed to strike us as rather odd. We exchanged glances. 'Doesn't it stop at Crewe?' asked one of us. 'No,' said our friend, briefly. He seemed almost disagreeable. There was a long pause. One of us, with a nod and a forced smile at the traveller, said 'Well!' The nod, the smile, and the unmeaning monosyllable, were returned conscientiously. Another pause was broken by one of us with a fit of coughing. It was an obviously assumed fit, but it served to pass the time. The bustle of the platform was unabated. There was no sign of the train's departure. Release—ours, and our friend's—was not yet.

My wandering eye alighted on a rather portly middle-aged man who was talking earnestly from the platform to a young lady at the next window but one to ours. His fine profile was vaguely familiar to me. The young lady was evidently American, and he was evidently English; otherwise I should have guessed from his impressive air that he was her father. I wished I could hear what he was saying. I was sure he was giving the very best advice; and the strong tenderness of his gaze was really beautiful. He seemed magnetic, as he poured out his final injunctions. I could feel something of his magnetism even where I stood. And the magnetism, like the profile, was vaguely familiar to me. Where had I experienced it?

In a flash I remembered. The man was Hubert le Ros. But how changed since last I saw him! That was seven or eight years ago, in the Strand. He was then (as usual) out of an engagement, and borrowed half-a-crown. It seemed a privilege to lend anything to him. He was always magnetic. And why his magnetism had never made him successful on the London stage was always a mystery to me. He was an excellent actor, and a man of sober habit. But, like many others of his kind, Hubert le Ros (I do not, of course, give the actual name by which he was known) drifted seedily away into the provinces; and I, like every one else, ceased to remember him.

It was strange to see him, after all these years, here on the platform of Euston, looking so prosperous and solid. It was not only the flesh that he had put on, but also the clothes, that made him hard to recognise. In the old days, an imitation fur coat had seemed to be as integral a part of him as were his ill-shorn lantern jaws. But now his costume was a model of rich and sombre moderation, drawing, not calling, attention to itself. He looked like a banker. Any one would have been proud to be seen off by him.

'Stand back, please.' The train was about to start, and I waved farewell to my friend. Le Ros did not stand back. He stood clasping in both hands the hands of the young American. 'Stand back, sir, please!' He obeyed, but quickly darted forward again to whisper some final word. I think there were tears in her eyes. There certainly were tears in his when, at length, having watched the train out of sight, he turned round. He seemed, nevertheless, delighted to see me. He asked me where I had been hiding all these years; and simultaneously repaid me the half-crown as though it had been borrowed yesterday. He linked his arm in mine, and walked me slowly along the platform, saying with what pleasure he read my dramatic criticisms every Saturday.

I told him, in return, how much he was missed on the stage. 'Ah, yes,' he said, 'I never act on the stage nowadays.' He laid some emphasis on the word 'stage,' and I asked him where, then, he did act. 'On the platform,' he answered. 'You mean,' said I, 'that you recite at concerts?' He smiled. 'This,' he whispered, striking his stick on the ground, 'is the platform I mean.' Had his mysterious prosperity unhinged him? He looked quite sane. I begged him to be more explicit.

'I suppose,' he said presently, giving me a light for the cigar which he had offered me, 'you have been seeing a friend off?' I assented. He asked me what I supposed he had been doing. I said that I had watched him doing the same thing. 'No,' he said gravely. 'That lady was not a friend of mine. I met her for the first time this morning, less than half an hour ago, here,' and again he struck the platform with his stick.

I confessed that I was bewildered. He smiled. 'You may,' he said, 'have heard of the Anglo-American Social Bureau?' I had not. He explained to me that of the thousands of Americans who annually pass through England there are many hundreds who have no English friends. In the old days they used to bring letters of introduction. But the English are so inhospitable that these letters are hardly worth the paper they are written on. 'Thus,' said Le Ros, 'the A.A.S.B. supplies a long-felt want. Americans are a sociable people, and most of them have plenty of money to spend. The A.A.S.B. supplies them with English friends. Fifty per cent. of the fees is paid over to the friends. The other fifty is retained by the A.A.S.B. I am not, alas, a director. If I were, I should be a very rich man indeed. I am only an employé. But even so I do very well. I am one of the seers-off.'

Again I asked for enlightenment. 'Many Americans,' he said, 'cannot afford to keep friends in England. But they can all afford to be seen off. The fee is only five pounds (twenty-five dollars) for a single traveller; and eight pounds (forty dollars) for a party of two or more. They send that in to the Bureau, giving the date of their departure, and a description by which the seer-off can identify them on the platform. And then—well, then they are seen off.'

'But is it worth it?' I exclaimed. 'Of course it is worth it,' said Le Ros. 'It prevents them from feeling "out of it." It earns them the respect of the guard.

It saves them from being despised by their fellow-passengers—the people who are going to be on the boat. It gives them a footing for the whole voyage. Besides, it is a great pleasure in itself. You saw me seeing that young lady off. Didn't you think I did it beautifully?' 'Beautifully,' I admitted. 'I envied you. There was I—' 'Yes, I can imagine. There were you, shuffling from foot to foot, staring blankly at your friend, trying to make conversation. I know. That's how I used to be myself, before I studied, and went into the thing professionally. I don't say I'm perfect yet. I'm still a martyr to platform fright. A railway station is the most difficult of all places to act in, as you have discovered for yourself.' 'But,' I said with resentment, 'I wasn't trying to act. I really felt.' 'So did I, my boy,' said Le Ros. 'You can't act without feeling. What's his name, the Frenchman—Diderot, yes—said you could; but what did he know about it? Didn't you see those tears in my eyes when the train started? I hadn't forced them. I tell you I was moved. So were you, I dare say. But you couldn't have pumped up a tear to prove it. You can't express your feelings. In other words, you can't act. At any rate,' he added kindly, 'not in a railway station.' 'Teach me!' I cried. He looked thoughtfully at me. 'Well,' he said at length, 'the seeing-off season is practically over. Yes, I'll give you a course. I have a good many pupils on hand already; but yes,' he said, consulting an ornate note-book, 'I could give you an hour on Tuesdays and Fridays.'

His terms, I confess, are rather high. But I don't grudge the investment.

A MEMORY OF A MIDNIGHT EXPRESS

Often I have presentiments of evil; but, never having had one of them fulfilled, I am beginning to ignore them. I find that I have always walked straight, serenely imprescient, into whatever trap Fate has laid for me. When I think of any horrible thing that has befallen me, the horror is intensified by recollection of its suddenness. 'But a moment before, I had been quite happy, quite secure. A moment later—' I shudder. Why be thus at Fate's mercy always, when with a little ordinary second sight...Yet no! That is the worst of a presentiment: it never averts evil, it does but unnerve the victim. Best, after all, to have only false presentiments like mine. Bolts that cannot be dodged strike us kindliest from the blue.

And so let me be thankful that my sole emotion as I entered an empty compartment at Holyhead was that craving for sleep which, after midnight, overwhelms every traveller—especially the Saxon traveller from tumultuous and quick-witted little Dublin. Mechanically, comfortably, as I sank into a corner, I rolled my rug round me, laid my feet against the opposite cushions, twitched up my coat collar above my ears, twitched down my cap over my eyes.

It was not the jerk of the starting train that half awoke me, but the consciousness that some one had flung himself into the compartment when the train was already in motion. I saw a small man putting something in the rack—a large black hand-bag. Through the haze of my sleep I saw him, vaguely resented him. He had no business to have slammed the door like that, no business to have jumped into a moving train, no business to put that huge hand-bag into a rack which was 'for light baggage only,' and no business to be wearing, at this hour and in this place, a top-hat. These four peevish objections floated sleepily together round my brain. It was not till the man turned round, and I met his eye, that I awoke fully—awoke to danger. I had never seen a murderer, but I knew that the man who was so steadfastly peering at me now...I shut my eyes. I tried to think. Could I be dreaming? In books I had read of people pinching themselves to see whether they were really awake. But in actual life there never was any doubt on that score. The great thing was that I should keep all my wits about me. Everything might depend on presence of mind. Perhaps this murderer was mad. If you fix a lunatic with your eye...

Screwing up my courage, I fixed the man with my eye. I had never seen such a horrible little eye as his. It was a sane eye, too. It radiated a cold and ruthless sanity. It belonged not to a man who would kill you wantonly, but to one who would not scruple to kill you for a purpose, and who would do the job quickly and neatly, and not be found out. Was he physically strong? Though he looked very wiry, he was little and narrow, like his eyes. He could not overpower me by force, I thought (and instinctively I squared my shoulders against the cushions, that he might realise the impossibility of overpowering me), but I felt he had enough 'science' to make me less than a match for him. I tried to look cunning and determined. I longed for a moustache like his, to hide my somewhat amiable mouth. I was thankful I could not see his mouth—could not know the worst of the face that was staring at me in the lamplight. And yet what could be worse than his eyes, gleaming from the deep shadow cast by the brim of his top-hat? What deadlier than that square jaw, with the bone so sharply delineated under the taut skin?

The train rushed on, noisily swaying through the silence of the night. I thought of the unseen series of placid landscapes that we were passing through, of the unconscious cottagers snoring there in their beds, of the safe people in the next compartment to mine—to his. Not moving a muscle, we sat there, we two, watching each other, like two hostile cats. Or rather, I thought, he watched me as a snake watches a rabbit, and I, like a rabbit, could not look away. I seemed to hear my heart beating time to the train. Suddenly my heart was at a standstill, and the double beat of the train receded faintly. The man was pointing upwards...I shook my head. He had asked me in a low voice, whether he should pull the hood across the lamp.

He was standing now with his back turned towards me, pulling his hand-bag out of the rack. He had a furtive back—the back of a man who, in his day, had borne many an alias. To this day I am ashamed that I did not spring up and pinion him, there and then. Had I possessed one ounce of physical courage, I should have done so. A coward, I let slip the opportunity. I thought of the communication-cord, but how could I move to it? He would be too quick for me. He would be very angry with me. I would sit quite still and wait. Every moment was a long reprieve to me now. Something might intervene to save me. There might be a collision on the line. Perhaps he was a quite harmless man...I caught his eyes, and shuddered...

His bag was open on his knees. His right hand was groping in it. (Thank Heaven he had not pulled the hood over the lamp!) I saw him pull out something—a limp thing, made of black cloth, not unlike the thing which a dentist places over your mouth when laughing-gas is to be administered. 'Laughing-gas, no laughing matter'—the irrelevant and idiotic embryo of a pun dangled itself for an instant in my brain. What other horrible thing would come out of the bag? Perhaps some gleaming instrument?... He closed the bag with a snap, laid it beside him. He took off his top-hat, laid that beside him. I was surprised (I know not why) to see that he was bald. There was a gleaming high light on his bald, round head. The limp, black thing was a cap, which he slowly adjusted with both hands, drawing it down over the brow and behind the ears. It seemed to me as though he were, after all, hooding the lamp; in my feverish fancy the compartment grew darker when the orb of his head was hidden. The shadow of another simile for his action came surging up... He had put on the cap so gravely, so judicially. Yes, that was it: he had assumed the black cap, that decent symbol which indemnifies the taker of a life; and might the Lord have mercy on my soul... Already he was addressing me... What had he said? I asked him to repeat it. My voice sounded even further away than his. He repeated that he thought we had met before. I heard my voice saying politely, somewhere in the distance, that I thought not. He suggested that I had been staying at some hotel in Colchester six years ago. My voice, drawing a little nearer to me, explained that I had never in my life been at Colchester. He begged my pardon and hoped no offence would be taken where none had been meant. My voice, coming right back to its own quarters, reassured him that of course I had taken no offence at all, adding that I myself very often mistook one face for another. He replied, rather inconsequently, that the world was a small place.

Evidently he must have prepared this remark to follow my expected admission that I had been at that hotel in Colchester six years ago, and have thought it too striking a remark to be thrown away. A guileless creature evidently, and not a criminal at all. Then I reflected that most of the successful criminals succeed rather through the incomparable guilelessness of the police than through any devilish cunning in themselves. Besides, this man looked the very incarnation of ruthless cunning. Surely, he must but have dissembled. My suspicions of him resurged. But somehow, I was no longer afraid of him. Whatever crimes he might have been committing, and be going to commit, I felt that he meant no harm to me. After all, why should I have imagined myself to be in danger? Meanwhile, I would try to draw the man out, pitting my wits against his.

I proceeded to do so. He was very voluble in a quiet way. Before long I was in possession of all the materials for an exhaustive biography of him. And the strange thing was that I could not, with the best will in the world, believe that he was lying to me. I had never heard a man telling so obviously the truth. And the truth about any one, however commonplace, must always be interesting. Indeed, it is the commonplace truth—the truth of widest application—that is the most interesting of all truths.

I do not now remember many details of this man's story; I remember merely that he was 'travelling in lace,' that he had been born at Boulogne (this was the one strange feature of the narrative), that somebody had once left him L100 in a will, and that he had a little daughter who was 'as pretty as a pink.' But at the time I was enthralled. Besides, I liked the man immensely. He was a kind and simple soul, utterly belying his appearance. I wondered how I ever could have feared him and hated him. Doubtless, the reaction from my previous state intensified the kindliness of my feelings. Anyhow, my heart went out to him. I felt that we had known each other for many years. While he poured out his recollections I felt that he was an old crony, talking over old days which were mine as well as his. Little by little, however, the slumber which he had scared from me came hovering back. My eyelids drooped; my comments on his stories became few and muffled. 'There!' he said, 'you're sleepy. I ought to have thought of that.' I protested feebly. He insisted kindly. 'You go to sleep,' he said, rising and drawing the hood over the lamp. It was dawn when I awoke. Some one in a top-hat was standing over me and saying 'Euston.' 'Euston?' I repeated. 'Yes, this is Euston. Good day to you.' 'Good day to you,' I repeated mechanically, in the grey dawn.

Not till I was driving through the cold empty streets did I remember the episode of the night, and who it was that had awoken me. I wished I could see my friend again. It was horrible to think that perhaps I should never see him again. I had liked him so much, and he had seemed to like me. I should not have said that he was a happy man. There was something melancholy about him. I hoped he would prosper. I had a foreboding that some great calamity was in store for him, and wished I could avert it. I thought of his little daughter who was 'as pretty as a pink.' Perhaps Fate was going to strike him through her. Perhaps when he got home he would find that she was dead. There were tears in my eyes when I alighted on my doorstep.

Thus, within a little space of time, did I experience two deep emotions, for neither of which was there any real justification. I experienced terror, though there was nothing to be afraid of, and I experienced sorrow, though there was nothing at all to be sorry about. And both my terror and my sorrow were, at the time, overwhelming.

You have no patience with me? Examine yourselves. Examine one another. In every one of us the deepest emotions are constantly caused by some absurdly trivial thing, or by nothing at all. Conversely, the great things in our lives—the true occasions for wrath, anguish, rapture, what not—very often leave us quite calm. We never can depend on any right adjustment of emotion to circumstance. That is one of many reasons which prevent the philosopher from taking himself and his fellow-beings quite so seriously as he would wish.

PORRO UNUM...

By graceful custom, every newcomer to a throne in Europe pays a round of visits to his neighbours. When King Edward came back from seeing the Tsar at Reval, his subjects seemed to think that he had fulfilled the last demand on his civility. That was in the days of Abdul Hamid. None of us wished the King to visit Turkey. Turkey is not internationally powerful, nor had Abdul any Guelph blood in him; and so we were able to assert, by ignoring her and him, our humanitarianism and passion for liberty, quite safely, quite politely. Now that Abdul is deposed from 'his infernal throne,' it is taken as a matter of course that the King will visit his successor. Well, let His Majesty betake himself and his tact and a full cargo of Victorian Orders to Constantinople, by all means. But, on the way, nestling in the very heart of Europe, perfectly civilised and strifeless, jewelled all over with freedom, is another country which he has not visited since his accession—a country which, oddly enough, none but I seems to expect him to visit. Why, I ask, should Switzerland be cold-shouldered?

I admit she does not appeal to the romantic imagination. She never has, as a nation, counted for anything. Physically soaring out of sight, morally and intellectually she has lain low and said nothing. Not one idea, not one deed, has she to her credit. All that is worth knowing of her history can be set forth without compression in a few lines of a guide-book. Her one and only hero—William Tell—never, as we now know, existed. He has been proved to be a myth. Also, he is the one and only myth that Switzerland has managed to create. He exhausted her poor little stock of imagination. Living as pigmies among the blind excesses of Nature, living on sufferance there, animalculae, her sons have been overwhelmed from the outset, have had no chance whatsoever of development. Even if they had a language of their own, they would have no literature. Not one painter, not one musician, have they produced; only couriers, guides, waiters, and other parasites. A smug, tame, sly, dull, mercenary little race of men, they exist by and for the alien tripper. They are the fine flower of commercial civilisation, the shining symbol of international comity, and have never done anybody any harm. I cannot imagine why the King should not give them the incomparable advertisement of a visit.

Not that they are badly in need of advertisement over here. Every year the British trippers to Switzerland vastly outnumber the British trippers to any other land—a fact which shows how little the romantic imagination tells as against cheapness and comfort of hotels and the notion that a heart strained by climbing is good for the health. And this fact does but make our Sovereign's abstention the more remarkable. Switzerland is not 'smart,' but a King is not the figure-head merely of his entourage: he is the whole nation's figure-head. Switzerland, alone among nations, is a British institution, and King Edward ought not to snub her. That we expect him to do so without protest from us, seems to me a rather grave symptom of flunkeyism.

Fiercely resenting that imputation, you proceed to raise difficulties. 'Who,' you ask, 'would there be to receive the King in the name of the Swiss nation?' I promptly answer, 'The President of the Swiss Republic.' You did not expect that. You had quite forgotten, if indeed you had ever heard, that there was any such person. For the life of you, you could not tell me his name. Well, his name is not very widely known even in Switzerland. A friend of mine, who was there lately, tells me that he asked one Swiss after another what was the name of the President, and that they all sought refuge in polite astonishment at such ignorance, and, when pressed for the name, could only screw up their eyes, snap their fingers, and feverishly declare that they had it on the tips of their tongues. This is just as it should be. In an ideal republic there should be no one whose name might not at any moment slip the memory of his fellows. Some sort of foreman there must be, for the State's convenience; but the more obscure he be, and the more automatic, the better for the ideal of equality. In the Republics of France and of America the President is of an extrusive kind. His office has been fashioned on the monarchic model, and his whole position is anomalous. He has to try to be ornamental as well as useful, a symbol as well as a pivot. Obviously, it is absurd to single out one man as a symbol of the equality of all men. And not less unreasonable is it to expect him to be inspiring as a patriotic symbol, an incarnation of his country. Only an anointed king, whose forefathers were kings too, can be that. In France, where kings have been, no one can get up the slightest pretence of emotion for the President. If the President is modest and unassuming, and doesn't, as did the late M. Faure, make an ass of himself by behaving in a kingly manner, he is safe from ridicule: the amused smiles that follow him are not unkind. But in no case is any one proud of him. Never does any one see France in him. In America, where no kings have been, they are able to make a pretence of enthusiasm for a President. But no real chord of national sentiment is touched by this eminent gentleman who has no past or future eminence, who has been shoved forward for a space and will anon be sent packing in favour of some other upstart. Let some princeling of a foreign State set foot in America, and lo! all the inhabitants are tumbling over one another in their desire for a glimpse of him—a desire which is the natural and pathetic outcome of their unsatisfied inner craving for a dynasty of their own. Human nature being what it is, a monarchy is the best expedient, all the world over. But, given a republic, let the thing be done thoroughly, let the appearance be well kept up, as in Switzerland. Let the President be, as there, a furtive creature and insignificant, not merely coming no man knows whence, nor merely passing no man knows whither, but existing no man knows where; and existing not even as a name—except on the tip of the tongue. National dignity, as well as the republican ideal, is served better thus. Besides, it is less trying for the President.

And yet, stronger than all my sense of what is right and proper is the desire in me that the President of the Swiss Republic should, just for once, be dragged forth, blinking, from his burrow in Berne (Berne is the capital of Switzerland), into the glare of European publicity, and be driven in a landau to the railway station, there to await the King of England and kiss him on either cheek when he dismounts from the train, while the massed orchestras of all the principal hotels play our national anthem—and also a Swiss national anthem, hastily composed for the occasion. I want him to entertain the King, that evening, at a great banquet, whereat His Majesty will have the President's wife on his right hand, and will make a brief but graceful speech in the Swiss language (English, French, German, and Italian, consecutively) referring to the glorious and never-to-be-forgotten name of William Tell (embarrassed silence), and to the vast number of his subjects who annually visit Switzerland (loud and prolonged cheers). Next morning, let there be a review of twenty thousand waiters from all parts of the country, all the head-waiters receiving a modest grade of the Victorian Order. Later in the day, let the King visit the National Gallery—a hall filled with picture post-cards of the most picturesque spots in Switzerland; and thence let him be conducted to the principal factory of cuckoo-clocks, and, after some of the clocks have been made to strike, be heard remarking to the President, with a hearty laugh, that the sound is like that of the cuckoo. How the second day of the visit would be filled up, I do not know; I leave that to the President's discretion. Before his departure to the frontier, the King will of course be made honorary manager of one of the principal hotels.

I hope to be present in Berne during these great days in the President's life. But, if anything happen to keep me here, I shall content myself with the prospect of his visit to London. I long to see him and his wife driving past, with the proper escort of Life Guards, under a vista of quadrilingual mottoes, bowing acknowledgments to us. I wonder what he is like. I picture him as a small spare man, with a slightly grizzled beard, and pleasant though shifty eyes behind a pince-nez. I picture him frock-coated, bowler-hatted, and evidently nervous. His wife I cannot at all imagine.

A CLUB IN RUINS

An antique ruin has its privileges. The longer the period of its crumbling, the more do the owls build their nests in it, the more do the excursionists munch in it their sandwiches. Thus, year by year, its fame increases, till it looks back with contempt on the days when it was a mere upright waterproof. Local guide-books pander more and more slavishly to its pride; leader-writers in need of a pathetic metaphor are more and more frequently supplied by it. If there be any sordid question of clearing it away to make room for something else, the public outcry is positively deafening.

Not that we are still under the sway of that peculiar cult which beset us in the earlier part of the nineteenth century. A bad poet or painter can no longer reap the reward of genius merely by turning his attention to ruins under moonlight. Nor does any one cause to be built in his garden a broken turret, for the evocation of sensibility in himself and his guests. There used to be one such turret near the summit of Campden Hill; but that familiar imposture was rased a year or two ago, no one protesting. Fuit the frantic factitious sentimentalism for ruins. On the other hand, the sentiment for them is as strong as ever it was. Decrepit Carisbrooke and its rivals annually tighten their hold on Britannia's heart.

I do not grudge them their success. But the very fact that they are so successful inclines me to reserve my own personal sentiment rather for those unwept, unsung ruins which so often confront me, here and there, in the streets of this aggressive metropolis. The ruins made, not by Time, but by the ruthless skill of Labour, the ruins of houses not old enough to be sacrosanct nor new enough to keep pace with the demands of a gasping and plethoric community—these are the ruins that move me to tears. No owls flutter in them. No trippers lunch in them. In no guide-book or leading-article will you find them mentioned. Their pathetic interiors gape to the sky and to the street, but nor gods nor men hold out a hand to save them. The patterns of bedroom wall-papers, (chosen with what care, after how long discussion! only a few short years or months ago) stare out their obvious, piteous appeal to us for mercy. And their dumb agony is echoed dumbly by the places where doors have been—doors that lately were tapped at by respectful knuckles; or the places where staircases have been—staircases down whose banisters lately slid little children, laughing. Exposed, humiliated, doomed, the home throws out a hundred pleas to us. And the Pharisaic community passes by on the other side of the way, in fear of a falling brick. Down come the walls of the home, as quickly as pickaxes can send them. Down they crumble, piecemeal, into the foundations, and are carted away. Soon other walls will be rising—red-brick 'residential' walls, more in harmony with the Zeitgeist. None but I pays any heed to the ruins.

I am their only friend. Me they attract so irresistibly that I haunt the door of the hoarding that encloses them, and am frequently mistaken for the foreman.

A few summers ago, I was watching, with more than usual emotion, the rasure of a great edifice at a corner of Hanover Square. There were two reasons why this rasure especially affected me. I had known the edifice so well, by sight, ever since I was a small boy, and I had always admired it as a fine example of that kind of architecture which is the most suitable to London's atmosphere. Though I must have passed it thousands of times, I had never passed without an upward smile of approval that gaunt and sombre facade, with its long straight windows, its well-spaced columns, its long straight coping against the London sky. My eyes deplored that these noble and familiar things must perish. For sake of what they had sheltered, my heart deplored that they must perish. The falling edifice had not been exactly a home. It had been even more than that. It had been a refuge from many homes. It had been a club.

Certainly it had not been a particularly distinguished club. Its demolition could not have been stayed on the plea that Charles James Fox had squandered his substance in its card-room, or that Lord Melbourne had loved to doze on the bench in its hall. Nothing sublime had happened in it. No sublime person had belonged to it. Persons without the vaguest pretensions to sublimity had always, I believe, found quick and easy entrance into it. It had been a large nondescript affair. But (to adapt Byron) a club's a club tho' every one's in it. The ceremony of election gives it a cachet which not even the smartest hotel has. And then there is the note-paper, and there are the newspapers, and the cigars at wholesale prices, and the not-to-be-tipped waiters, and other blessings for mankind. If the members of this club had but migrated to some other building, taking their effects and their constitution with them, the ruin would have been pathetic enough. But alas! the outward wreck was a symbol, a result, of inner dissolution. Through the door of the hoarding the two pillars of the front door told a sorry tale. Pasted on either of them was a dingy bill, bearing the sinister imprimatur of an auctioneer, and offering (in capitals of various sizes) Bedroom Suites (Walnut and Mahogany), Turkey, Indian and Wilton Pile Carpets, Two Full-sized Billiard-Tables, a Remington Type-writer, a Double Door (Fire-Proof), and other objects not less useful and delightful. The club, then, had gone to smash. The members had been disbanded, driven out of this Eden by the fiery sword of the Law, driven back to their homes. Sighing over the marcescibility of human happiness, I peered between the pillars into the excavated and chaotic hall. The porter's hatch was still there, in the wall. There it was, wondering why no inquiries were made through it now, or, may be, why it had not been sold into bondage with the double-door and the rest of the fixtures. A melancholy relic of past glories! I crossed over to the other side of the road, and passed my eye over the whole ruin. The roof, the ceilings, most of the inner walls, had already fallen. Little remained but the grim, familiar facade—a thin husk. I noted (that which I had never noted before) two iron grills in the masonry. Miserable travesties of usefulness, ventilating the open air! Through the gaping windows, against the wall of the next building, I saw in mid-air the greenish Lincrusta Walton of what I guessed to have been the billiard-room—the billiard-room that had boasted two full-sized tables. Above it ran a frieze of white and gold. It was interspersed with flat Corinthian columns. The gilding of the capitals was very fresh, and glittered gaily under the summer sunbeams.

And hardly a day of the next autumn and winter passed but I was drawn back to the ruin by a kind of lugubrious magnetism. The strangest thing was that the ruin seemed to remain in practically the same state as when first I had come upon it: the facade still stood high. This might have been due to the proverbial laziness of British workmen, but I did not think it could be. The workmen were always plying their pick-axes, with apparent gusto and assiduity, along the top of the building; bricks and plaster were always crashing down into the depths and sending up clouds of dust. I preferred to think the building renewed itself, by some magical process, every night. I preferred to think it was prepared thus to resist its aggressors for so long a time that in the end there would be an intervention from other powers. Perhaps from this site no 'residential' affair was destined to scrape the sky? Perhaps that saint to whom the club had dedicated itself would reappear, at length, glorious equestrian, to slay the dragons who had infested and desecrated his premises? I wondered whether he would then restore the ruins, reinstating the club, and setting it for ever on a sound commercial basis, or would leave them just as they were, a fixed signal to sensibility.

But, when first I saw the poor facade being pick-axed, I did not 'give' it more than a fortnight. I had no feeling but of hopeless awe and pity. The workmen on the coping seemed to me ministers of inexorable Olympus, executing an Olympian decree. And the building seemed to me a live victim, a scapegoat suffering sullenly for sins it had not committed. To me it seemed to be flinching under every rhythmic blow of those well-wielded weapons, praying for the hour when sunset should bring it surcease from that daily ordeal. I caught myself nodding to it—a nod of sympathy, of hortation to endurance. Immediately, I was ashamed of my lapse into anthropomorphism. I told myself that my pity ought to be kept for the real men who had been frequenters of the building, who now were waifs. I reviewed the gaping, glassless windows through which they had been wont to watch the human comedy. There they had stood, puffing their smoke and cracking their jests, and tearing women's reputations to shreds.

Not that I, personally, have ever heard a woman's reputation torn to shreds in a club window. A constant reader of lady-novelists, I have always been hoping for this excitement, but somehow it has never come my way. I am beginning to suspect that it never will, and am inclined to regard it as a figment. Such conversation as I have heard in clubs has been always of a very mild, perfunctory kind. A social club (even though it be a club with a definite social character) is a collection of heterogeneous creatures, and its aim is perfect harmony and good-fellowship. Thus any definite expression of opinion by any member is regarded as dangerous. The ideal clubman is he who looks genial and says nothing at all. Most Englishmen find little difficulty in conforming with this ideal. They belong to a silent race. Social clubs flourish, therefore, in England. Intelligent foreigners, seeing them, recognise their charm, and envy us them, and try to reproduce them at home. But the Continent is too loquacious. On it social clubs quickly degenerate into bear-gardens, and the basic ideal of good-fellowship goes by the board. In Paris, Petersburg, Vienna, the only social clubs that prosper are those which are devoted to games of chance—those which induce silence by artificial means. Were I a foreign visitor, taking cursory glances, I should doubtless be delighted with the clubs of London. Had I the honour to be an Englishman, I should doubtless love them. But being a foreign resident, I am somewhat oppressed by them. I crave in them a little freedom of speech, even though such freedom were their ruin. I long for their silence to be broken here and there, even though such breakage broke them with it. It is not enough for me to hear a hushed exchange of mild jokes about the weather, or of comparisons between what the Times says and what the Standard says. I pine for a little vivacity, a little boldness, a little variety, a few gestures. A London club, as it is conducted, seems to me very like a catacomb. It is tolerable so long as you do not actually belong to it. But when you do belong to it, when you have outlived the fleeting gratification at having been elected, when you...but I ought not to have fallen into the second person plural. You, readers, are free-born Englishmen. These clubs 'come natural' to you. You love them. To them you slip eagerly from your homes. As for me, poor alien, had I been a member of the club whose demolition has been my theme, I should have grieved for it not one whit the more bitterly. Indeed, my tears would have been a trifle less salt. It was my detachment that enabled me to be so prodigal of pity.

The poor waifs! Long did I stand, in the sunshine of that day when first I saw the ruin, wondering and distressed, ruthful, indignant that such things should be. I forgot on what errand I had come out. I recalled it. Once or twice I walked away, bent on its fulfilment. But I could not proceed further than a few yards. I halted, looked over my shoulder, was drawn back to the spot, drawn by the crude, insistent anthem of the pick-axes. The sun slanted towards Notting Hill. Still I loitered, spellbound... I was aware of some one at my side, some one asking me a question. 'I beg your pardon?' I said. The stranger was a tall man, bronzed and bearded. He repeated his question. In answer, I pointed silently to the ruin. 'That?' he gasped. He stared vacantly. I saw that his face had become pale under its sunburn. He looked from the ruin to me. 'You're not joking with me?' he said thickly. I assured him that I was not. I assured him that this was indeed the club to which he had asked to be directed. 'But,' he stammered, 'but—but—' 'You were a member?' I suggested. 'I am a member,' he cried. 'And what's more, I'm going to write to the Committee.' I suggested that there was one fatal objection to such a course. I spoke to him calmly, soothed him with words of reason, elicited from him, little by little, his sad story. It appeared that he had been a member of the club for ten years, but had never (except once, as a guest) been inside it. He had been elected on the very day on which (by compulsion of his father) he set sail for Australia. He was a mere boy at the time. Bitterly he hated leaving old England; nor did he ever find the life of a squatter congenial. The one thing which enabled him to endure those ten years of unpleasant exile was the knowledge that he was a member of a London club. Year by year, it was a keen pleasure to him to send his annual subscription. It kept him in touch with civilisation, in touch with Home. He loved to know that when, at length, he found himself once again in the city of his birth he would have a firm foothold on sociability. The friends of his youth might die, or might forget him. But, as member of a club, he would find substitutes for them in less than no time. Herding bullocks, all day long, on the arid plains of Central Australia, he used to keep up his spirits by thinking of that first whisky-and-soda which he would order from a respectful waiter as he entered his club. All night long, wrapped in his blanket beneath the stars, he used to dream of that drink to come, that first symbol of an unlost grip on civilisation... He had arrived in London this very afternoon. Depositing his luggage at an hotel, he had come straight to his club. 'And now...' He filled up his aposiopesis with an uncouth gesture, signifying 'I may as well get back to Australia.'

I was on the point of offering to take him to my own club and give him his first whisky-and-soda therein. But I refrained. The sight of an extant club might have maddened the man. It certainly was very hard for him, to have belonged to a club for ten years, to have loved it so passionately from such a distance, and then to find himself destined never to cross its threshold. Why, after all, should he not cross its threshold? I asked him if he would like to. 'What,' he growled, 'would be the good?' I appealed, not in vain, to the imaginative side of his nature. I went to the door of the hoarding, and explained matters to the foreman; and presently, nodding to me solemnly, he passed with the foreman through the gap between the doorposts. I saw him crossing the excavated hall, crossing it along a plank, slowly and cautiously. His attitude was very like Blondin's, but it had a certain tragic dignity which

Blondin's lacked. And that was the last I saw of him. I hailed a cab and drove away. What became of the poor fellow I do not know. Often as I returned to the ruin, and long as I loitered by it, him I never saw again. Perhaps he really did go straight back to Australia. Or perhaps he induced the workmen to bury him alive in the foundations. His fate, whatever it was, haunts me.

'273'

This is an age of prescriptions. Morning after morning, from the back-page of your newspaper, quick and uncostly cures for every human ill thrust themselves wildly on you. The age of miracles is not past. But I would raise no false hopes of myself. I am no thaumaturgist. Do you awake with a sinking sensation in the stomach? Have you lost the power of assimilating food? Are you oppressed with an indescribable lassitude? Can you no longer follow the simplest train of thought? Are you troubled throughout the night with a hacking cough? Are you—in fine, are you but a tissue of all the most painful symptoms of all the most malignant maladies ancient and modern? If so, skip this essay, and try Somebody's Elixir. The cure that I offer is but a cure for overwrought nerves—a substitute for the ordinary 'rest-cure.' Nor is it absurdly cheap. Nor is it instant. It will take a week or so of your time. But then, the 'rest-cure' takes at least a month. The scale of payment for board and lodging may be, per diem, hardly lower than in the 'rest-cure'; but you will save all but a pound or so of the very heavy fees that you would have to pay to your doctor and your nurse (or nurses). And certainly, my cure is the more pleasant of the two. My patient does not have to cease from life. He is not undressed and tucked into bed and forbidden to stir hand or foot during his whole term. He is not forbidden to receive letters, or to read books, or to look on any face but his nurse's (or nurses'). Nor, above all, is he condemned to the loathsome necessity of eating so much food as to make him dread the sight of food. Doubtless, the grim, inexorable process of the 'rest-cure' is very good for him who is strong enough and brave enough to bear it, and rich enough to pay for it. I address myself to the frailer, cowardlier, needier man. Instead of ceasing from life, and entering purgatory, he need but essay a variation in life. He need but go and stay by himself in one of those vast modern hotels which abound along the South and East coasts.

You are disappointed? All simple ideas are disappointing. And all good cures spring from simple ideas.

The right method of treating overwrought nerves is to get the patient away from himself—to make a new man of him; and this trick can be done only by switching him off from his usual environment, his usual habits. The ordinary rest-cure, by its very harshness, intensifies a man's personality at first, drives him miserably within himself; and only by its long duration does it gradually wear him down and build him up anew. There is no harshness in the vast hotels which I have recommended. You may eat there as little as you like, especially if you are en pension. Letters may be forwarded to you there; though, unless your case is a very mild one, I would advise you not to leave your address at home. There are reading-rooms where you can see all the newspapers; though I advise you to ignore them. You suffer under no sense of tyranny. And yet, no sooner have you signed your name in the visitors' book, and had your bedroom allotted to you, than you feel that you have surrendered yourself irrepleviably. It is not necessary to this illusion that you should pass under an assumed name, unless you happen to be a very eminent actor, or cricketer, or other idol of the nation, whose presence would flutter the young persons at the bureau. If your nervous breakdown be (as it more likely is) due to merely intellectual distinction, these young persons will mete out to you no more than the bright callous civility which they mete out impartially to all (but those few) who come before them. To them you will be a number, and to yourself you will have suddenly become a number—the number graven on the huge brass label that depends clanking from the key put into the hand of the summoned chambermaid. You are merely (let us say) 273.

Up you go in the lift, realising, as for the first time, your insignificance in infinity, and rather proud to be even a number. You recognise your double on the door that has been unlocked for you. No prisoner, clapped into his cell, could feel less personal, less important. A notice on the wall, politely requesting you to leave your key at the bureau (as though you were strong enough or capacious enough to carry it about with you) comes as a pleasant reminder of your freedom. You remember joyously that you are even free from yourself. You have begun a new life, have forgotten the old. This mantelpiece, so strangely and brightly bare of photographs or 'knickknacks,' is meaning in its meaninglessness. And these blank, fresh walls, that you have never seen, and that never were seen by any one whom you know...their pattern is of poppies and mandragora, surely. Poppies and mandragora are woven, too, on the brand-new Axminster beneath your elastic step. 'Come in!' A porter bears in your trunk, deposits it on a trestle at the foot of the bed, unstraps it, leaves you alone with it. It seems to be trying to remind you of something or other. You do not listen. You laugh as you open it. You know that if you examined these shirts you would find them marked '273.' Before dressing for dinner, you take a hot bath. There are patent taps, some for fresh water, others for sea water. You hesitate. Yet you know that whichever you touch will effuse but the water of Lethe, after all. You dress before your fire. The coals have burnt now to a lovely glow. Once and again, you eye them suspiciously. But no, there are no faces in them. All's well.

Sleek and fresh, you sit down to dinner in the 'Grande Salle a' Manger.' Graven on your wine-glasses, emblazoned on your soup-plate, are the armorial bearings of the company that shelters you. The College of Arms might sneer at them, be down on them, but to you they are a joy, in their grand lack of links with history. They are a sympathetic symbol of your own newness, your own impersonality. You glance down the endless menu. It has been composed for a community. None of your favourite dishes (you once had favourite dishes) appears in it, thank heaven! You will work your way through it, steadily, unquestioningly, gladly, with a communal palate. And the wine? All wines are alike here, surely. You scour the list vaguely, and order a pint of 273. Your eye roves over the adjacent tables.

You behold a galaxy of folk evidently born, like yourself, anew. Some, like yourself, are solitary. Others are with wives, with children—but with new wives, new children. The associations of home have been forgotten, even though home's actual appendages be here. The members of the little domestic circles are using company manners. They are actually making conversation, 'breaking the ice.' They are new here to one another. They are new to themselves. How much newer to you! You cannot 'place' them. That paterfamilias with the red moustache—is he a soldier, a solicitor, a stockbroker, what? You play vaguely, vainly, at the game of attributions, while the little orchestra in yonder bower of artificial palm-trees plays new, or seemingly new, cake-walks. Who are they, these minstrels in the shadow? They seem not to be the Red Hungarians, nor the Blue, nor the Hungarians of any other colour of the spectrum. You set them down as the Colourless Hungarians, and resume your study of the tables. They fascinate you, these your fellow-diners. You fascinate them, doubtless. They, doubtless, are cudgelling their brains to 'spot' your state in life—your past, which now has escaped you. Next day, some of them are gone; and you miss them, almost bitterly. But others succeed them, not less detached and enigmatic than they. You must never speak to one of them. You must never lapse into those casual acquaintances of the 'lounge' or the smoking-room. Nor is it hard to avoid them. No Englishman, how gregarious and garrulous soever, will dare address another Englishman in whose eye is no spark of invitation. There must be no such spark in yours. Silence is part of the cure for you, and a very important part. It is mainly through unaccustomed silence that your nerves are made trim again. Usually, you are giving out in talk all that you receive through your senses of perception. Keep silence now. Its gold will accumulate in you at compound interest. You will realise the joy of being full of reflections and ideas. You will begin to hoard them proudly, like a miser. You will gloat over your own cleverness—you, who but a few days since, were feeling so stupid. Solitude in a crowd, silence among chatterboxes— these are the best ministers to a mind diseased. And with the restoration of the mind, the body will be restored too. You, who were physically so limp and pallid, will be a ruddy Hercules now. And when, at the moment of departure, you pass through the hall, shyly distributing to the servants that largesse which is so slight in comparison with what your doctor and nurse (or nurses) would have levied on you, you will feel that you are more than fit to resume that burden of personality whereunder you had sunk. You will be victoriously yourself again.

Yet I think you will look back a little wistfully on the period of your obliteration. People—for people are very nice, really, most of them—will tell you that they have missed you. You will reply that you did not miss yourself. And you will go the more strenuously to your work and pleasure, so as to have the sooner an excuse for a good riddance.

A STUDY IN DEJECTION

Riderless the horse was, and with none to hold his bridle. But he waited patiently, submissively, there where I saw him, at the shabby corner of a certain shabby little street in Chelsea. 'My beautiful, my beautiful, thou standest meekly by,' sang Mrs. Norton of her Arab steed, 'with thy proudly-arched and glossy neck, thy dark and fiery eye.' Catching the eye of this other horse, I saw that such fire as might once have blazed there had long smouldered away. Chestnut though he was, he had no mettle. His chestnut coat was all dull and rough, unkempt as that of an inferior cab-horse. Of his once luxuriant mane there were but a few poor tufts now. His saddle was torn and weather-stained. The one stirrup that dangled therefrom was red with rust.

I never saw in any creature a look of such unutterable dejection. Dejection, in the most literal sense of the word, indeed was his. He had been cast down. He had fallen from higher and happier things. With his 'arched neck,' and with other points which not neglect nor ill-usage could rob of their old grace, he had kept something of his fallen day about him. In the window of the little shop outside which he stood were things that seemed to match him—things appealing to the sense that he appealed to. A tarnished French mirror, a strip of faded carpet, some rows of battered, tattered books, a few cups and saucers that had erst been riveted and erst been dusted—all these, in a gallimaufry of other languid odds and ends, seen through this mud-splashed window, silently echoed the silent misery of the horse. They were remembering Zion. They had been beautiful once, and expensive, and well cared for, and admired, and coveted. And now...

They had, at least, the consolation of being indoors. Public laughing-stock though they were, they had a barrier of glass between themselves and the irreverent world. To be warm and dry, too, was something. Piteous, they could yet afford to pity the horse. He was more ludicrously, more painfully, misplaced than they. A real blood-horse that has done his work is rightly left in the open air—turned out into some sweet meadow or paddock. It would be cruel to make him spend his declining years inside a house, where no grass is. Is it less cruel that a fine old rocking-horse should be thrust from the nursery out into the open air, upon the pavement?

Perhaps some child had just given the horse a contemptuous shove in passing. For he was rocking gently when I chanced to see him. Nor did he cease to rock, with a slight creak upon the pavement, so long as I watched him. A particularly black and bitter north wind was blowing round the corner of the street. Perhaps it was this that kept the horse in motion. Boreas himself, invisible to my mortal eyes, may have been astride the saddle, lashing the tired old horse to this futile activity. But no, I think rather that the poor thing was rocking of his own accord, rocking to attract my attention. He saw in me a possible purchaser. He wanted to show me that he was still sound in wind and limb. Had I a small son at home? If so, here was the very mount for him. None of your frisky, showy, first-hand young brutes, on which no fond parent ought to risk his offspring's bones; but a sound, steady-going, well-mannered old hack with never a spark of vice in him! Such was the message that I read in the glassy eye fixed on me. The nostril of faded scarlet seemed for a moment to dilate and quiver. At last, at last, was some one going to inquire his price?

Once upon a time, in a far-off fashionable toy-shop, his price had been prohibitive; and he, the central attraction behind the gleaming shop-window, had plumed himself on his expensiveness. He had been in no hurry to be bought. It had seemed to him a good thing to stand there motionless, majestic, day after day, far beyond the reach of average purses, and having in his mien something of the frigid nobility of the horses on the Parthenon frieze, with nothing at all of their unreality. A coat of real chestnut hair, glossy, glorious! From end to end of the Parthenon frieze not one of the horses had that.

From end to end of the toy-shop that exhibited him not one of the horses was thus graced. Their flanks were mere wood, painted white, with arbitrary blotches of grey here and there. Miserable creatures! It was difficult to believe that they had souls. No wonder they were cheap, and 'went off,' as the shopman said, so quickly, whilst he stayed grandly on, cynosure of eyes that dared not hope for him. Into bondage they went off, those others, and would be worked to death, doubtless, by brutal little boys.

When, one fine day, a lady was actually not shocked by the price demanded for him, his pride was hurt. And when, that evening, he was packed in brown paper and hoisted to the roof of a four-wheeler, he faced the future fiercely. Who was this lady that her child should dare bestride him? With a biblical 'ha, ha,' he vowed that the child should not stay long in saddle: he must be thrown—badly—even though it was his seventh birthday. But this wicked intention vanished while the child danced around him in joy and wonder. Never yet had so many compliments been showered on him. Here, surely, was more the manner of a slave than of a master. And how lightly the child rode him, with never a tug or a kick! And oh, how splendid it was to be flying thus through the air! Horses were made to be ridden; and he had never before savoured the true joy of life, for he had never known his own strength and fleetness. Forward! Backward! Faster, faster! To floor! To ceiling! Regiments of leaden soldiers watched his wild career. Noah's quiet sedentary beasts gaped up at him in wonderment—as tiny to him as the gaping cows in the fields are to you when you pass by in an express train. This was life indeed!

He remembered Katafalto—remembered Eclipse and the rest nowhere. Aye, thought he, and even thus must Black Bess have rejoiced along the road to York. And Bucephalus, skimming under Alexander the plains of Asia, must have had just this glorious sense of freedom. Only less so! Not Pegasus himself can have flown more swiftly. Pegasus, at last, became a constellation in the sky. 'Some day,' reflected the rocking-horse, when the ride was over, 'I, too, shall die; and five stars will appear on the nursery ceiling.'

Alas for the vanity of equine ambition! I wonder by what stages this poor beast came down in the world. Did the little boy's father go bankrupt, leaving it to be sold in a 'lot' with the other toys? Or was it merely given away, when the little boy grew up, to a poor but procreative relation, who anon became poorer? I should like to think that it had been mourned. But I fear that whatever mourning there may have been for it must have been long ago discarded. The creature did not look as if it had been ridden in any recent decade. It looked as if it had almost abandoned the hope of ever being ridden again. It was but hoping against hope now, as it stood rocking there in the bleak twilight. Bright warm nurseries were for younger, happier horses. Still it went on rocking, to show me that it could rock.

The more sentimental a man is, the less is he helpful; the more loth is he to cancel the cause of his emotion. I did not buy the horse.

A few days later, passing that way, I wished to renew my emotion; but lo! the horse was gone. Had some finer person than I bought it?—towed it to the haven where it would be? Likelier, it had but been relegated to some mirky recess of the shop... I hope it has room to rock there.

A PATHETIC IMPOSTURE

Lord Rosebery once annoyed the Press by declaring that his ideal newspaper was one which should give its news without comment. Doubtless he was thinking of the commonweal. Yet a plea for no comments might be made, with equal force, in behalf of the commentators themselves. Occupations that are injurious to the persons engaged in them ought not to be encouraged. The writing of 'leaders' and 'notes' is one of these occupations. The practice of it, more than of any other, depends on, and fosters hypocrisy, worst of vices. In a sense, every kind of writing is hypocritical. It has to be done with an air of gusto, though no one ever yet enjoyed the act of writing. Even a man with a specific gift for writing, with much to express, with perfect freedom in choice of subject and manner of expression, with indefinite leisure, does not write with real gusto. But in him the pretence is justified: he has enjoyed thinking out his subject, he will delight in his work when it is done. Very different is the pretence of one who writes at top-speed, on a set subject, what he thinks the editor thinks the proprietor thinks the public thinks nice. If he happen to have a talent for writing, his work will be but the more painful, and his hypocrisy the greater. The chances are, though, that the talent has already been sucked out of him by Journalism, that vampire. To her, too, he will have forfeited any fervour he may have had, any learning, any gaiety. How can he, the jaded interpreter, hold any opinion, feel any enthusiasm?—without leisure, keep his mind in cultivation?—be sprightly to order, at unearthly hours in a whir-r-ring office? To order! Yes, sprightliness is compulsory there; so are weightiness, and fervour, and erudition. He must seem to abound in these advantages, or another man will take his place. He must disguise himself at all costs. But disguises are not easy to make; they require time and care, which he cannot afford. So he must snatch up ready-made disguises—unhook them, rather. He must know all the cant-phrases, the cant-references. There are very, very many of them, and belike it is hard to keep them all at one's finger-tips. But, at least, there is no difficulty in collecting them. Plod through the 'leaders' and 'notes' in half-a-dozen of the daily papers, and you will bag whole coveys of them.

Most of the morning papers still devote much space to the old-fashioned kind of 'leader,' in which the pretence is of weightiness, rather than of fervour, sprightliness, or erudition. The effect of weightiness is obtained simply by a stupendous disproportion of language to sense. The longest and most emphatic words are used for the simplest and most trivial statements, and they are always so elaborately qualified as to leave the reader with a vague impression that a very difficult matter, which he himself cannot make head or tail of, has been dealt with in a very judicial and exemplary manner.

A leader-writer would not, for instance, say—

Lord Rosebery has made a paradox.

He would say:—

Lord Rosebery

whether intentionally or otherwise, we leave our readers to decide,
or, with seeming conviction,
or, doubtless giving rein to the playful humour which is characteristic of him,

has

expressed a sentiment,
or, taken on himself to enunciate a theory,
or, made himself responsible for a dictum,

which,

we venture to assert,
or, we have little hesitation in declaring,
or, we may be pardoned for thinking,
or, we may say without fear of contradiction,

is

nearly akin to
or, not very far removed from

the paradoxical.

But I will not examine further the trick of weightiness—it takes up too much of my space. Besides, these long 'leaders' are a mere survival, and will soon disappear altogether. The 'notes' are the characteristic feature of the modern newspaper, and it is in them that the modern journalist displays his fervour, sprightliness, and erudition. 'Note'-writing, like chess, has certain recognised openings, e.g.:—

There is no new thing under the sun.
It is always the unexpected that happens.
Nature, as we know, abhors a vacuum.
The late Lord Coleridge once electrified his court by inquiring 'Who is Connie Gilchrist?'

And here are some favourite methods of conclusion:—

A mad world, my masters!
'Tis true 'tis pity, and pity 'tis 'tis true.
There is much virtue in that 'if.'

But that, as Mr. Kipling would say, is another story.
Si non e' vero, etc.

or (lighter style)

We fancy we recognise here the hand of Mr. Benjamin Trovato.

Not less inevitable are such parallelisms as:—

Like Topsy, perhaps it 'growed.'
Like the late Lord Beaconsfield on a famous occasion, 'on the side of the angels.'
Like Brer Rabbit, 'To lie low and say nuffin.'
Like Oliver Twist, 'To ask for more.'
Like Sam Weller's knowledge of London, 'extensive and peculiar.'
Like Napoleon, a believer in 'the big battalions.'

Nor let us forget Pyrrhic victory, Parthian dart, and Homeric laughter; quos deus vult and nil de mortuis; Sturm und Drang; masterly inactivity, unctuous rectitude, mute inglorious Miltons, and damned good-natured friends; the sword of Damocles, the thin edge of the wedge, the long arm of coincidence, and the soul of goodness in things evil; Hobson's choice, Frankenstein's monster, Macaulay's schoolboy, Lord Burleigh's nod, Sir Boyle Roche's bird, Mahomed's coffin, and Davy Jones's locker.

A melancholy catalogue, is it not? But it is less melancholy for you who read it here, than for them whose existence depends on it, who draw from it a desperate means of seeming to accomplish what is impossible. And yet these are the men who shrank in horror from Lord Rosebery's merciful idea. They ought to be saved despite themselves. Might not a short Act of Parliament be passed, making all comment in daily newspapers illegal? In a way, of course, it would be hard on the commentators. Having lost the power of independent thought, having sunk into a state of chronic dulness, apathy and insincerity, they could hardly, be expected to succeed in any of the ordinary ways of life. They could not compete with their fellow-creatures; no door but would be bolted if they knocked on it. What would become of them? Probably they would have to perish in what they would call 'what the late Lord Goschen would have called "splendid isolation."' But such an end were sweeter, I suggest to them, than the life they are leading.

THE DECLINE OF THE GRACES

Have you read The Young Lady's Book? You have had plenty of time to do so, for it was published in 1829. It was described by the two anonymous Gentlewomen who compiled it as 'A Manual for Elegant Recreations, Exercises, and Pursuits.' You wonder they had nothing better to think of? You suspect them of having been triflers? They were not, believe me. They were careful to explain, at the outset, that the Virtues of Character were what a young lady should most assiduously cultivate. They, in their day, labouring under the shadow of the eighteenth century, had somehow in themselves that high moral fervour which marks the opening of the twentieth century, and is said to have come in with Mr. George Bernard Shaw. But, unlike us, they were not concerned wholly with the inward and spiritual side of life. They cared for the material surface, too. They were learned in the frills and furbelows of things. They gave, indeed, a whole chapter to 'Embroidery.' Another they gave to 'Archery,' another to 'The Aviary,' another to 'The Escrutoire.' Young ladies do not now keep birds, nor shoot with bow and arrow; but they do still, in some measure, write letters; and so, for sake of historical comparison, let me give you a glance at 'The Escrutoire.' It is not light reading.

'For careless scrawls ye boast of no pretence;
Fair Russell wrote, as well as spoke, with sense.'

Thus is the chapter headed, with a delightful little wood engraving of 'Fair Russell,' looking pre-eminently sensible, at her desk, to prepare the reader for the imminent welter of rules for 'decorous composition.' Not that pedantry is approved. 'Ease and simplicity, an even flow of unlaboured diction, and an artless arrangement of obvious sentiments' is the ideal to be striven for. 'A metaphor may be used with advantage' by any young lady, but only 'if it occur naturally.' And 'allusions are elegant,' but only 'when introduced with ease, and when they are well understood by those to whom they are addressed.' 'An antithesis renders a passage piquant'; but the dire results of a too-frequent indulgence in it are relentlessly set forth. Pages and pages are devoted to a minute survey of the pit-falls of punctuation. But when the young lady of that period had skirted all these, and had observed all the manifold rules of caligraphy that were here laid down for her, she was not, even then, out of the wood. Very special stress was laid on 'the use of the seal.' Bitter scorn was poured on young ladies who misused the seal. 'It is a habit of some to thrust the wax into the flame of the candle, and the moment a morsel of it is melted, to daub it on the paper; and when an unsightly mass is gathered together, to pass the seal over the tongue with ridiculous haste—press it with all the strength which the sealing party possesses—and the result is, an impression which raises a blush on her cheek.'

Well! The young ladies of that day were ever expected to exhibit sensibility, and used to blush, just as they wept or fainted, for very slight causes. Their tears and their swoons did not necessarily betoken much grief or agitation; nor did a rush of colour to the cheek mean necessarily that they were overwhelmed with shame. To exhibit various emotions in the drawing-room was one of the Elegant Exercises in which these young ladies were drilled thoroughly. And their habit of simulation was so rooted in sense of duty that it merged into sincerity. If a young lady did not swoon at the breakfast-table when her Papa read aloud from The Times that the Duke of Wellington was suffering from a slight chill, the chances were that she would swoon quite unaffectedly when she realised her omission. Even so, we may be sure that a young lady whose cheek burned not at sight of the letter she had sealed untidily—'unworthily' the Manual calls it—would anon be blushing for her shamelessness. Such a thing as the blurring of the family crest, or as the pollution of the profile of Pallas Athene with the smoke of the taper, was hardly, indeed, one of those 'very slight causes' to which I have referred. The Georgian young lady was imbued through and through with the sense that it was her duty to be gracefully efficient in whatsoever she set her hand to. To the young lady of to-day, belike, she will seem accordingly ridiculous—seem poor-spirited, and a pettifogger. True, she set her hand to no grandiose tasks. She was not allowed to become a hospital nurse, for example, or an actress. The young lady of to-day, when she hears in herself a 'vocation' for tending the sick, would willingly, without an instant's preparation, assume responsibility for the lives of a whole ward at St. Thomas's. This responsibility is not, however, thrust on her. She has to submit to a long and tedious course of training before she may do so much as smooth a pillow. The boards of the theatre are less jealously hedged in than those of the hospital. If our young lady have a wealthy father, and retain her schoolroom faculty for learning poetry by heart, there is no power on earth to prevent her from making her de'but, somewhere, as Juliet—if she be so inclined; and such is usually her inclination. That her voice is untrained, that she cannot scan blank-verse, that she cannot gesticulate with grace and propriety, nor move with propriety and grace across the stage, matters not a little bit—to our young lady. 'Feeling,' she will say, 'is everything'; and, of course, she, at the age of eighteen, has more feeling than Juliet, that 'flapper,' could have had. All those other things—those little technical tricks—'can be picked up,' or 'will come.' But no; I misrepresent our young lady. If she be conscious that there are such tricks to be played, she despises them. When, later, she finds the need to learn them, she still despises them. It seems to her ridiculous that one should not speak and comport oneself as artlessly on the stage as one does off it. The notion of speaking or comporting oneself with conscious art in real life would seem to her quite monstrous. It would puzzle her as much as her grandmother would have been puzzled by the contrary notion.

Personally, I range myself on the grandmother's side. I take my stand shoulder to shoulder with the Graces. On the banner that I wave is embroidered a device of prunes and prisms.

I am no blind fanatic, however. I admit that artlessness is a charming idea. I admit that it is sometimes charming as a reality. I applaud it (all the more heartily because it is rare) in children. But then, children, like the young of all animals whatsoever, have a natural grace. As a rule, they begin to show it in their third year, and to lose it in their ninth. Within that span of six years they can be charming without intention; and their so frequent failure in charm is due to their voluntary or enforced imitation of the ways of their elders. In Georgian and Early Victorian days the imitation was always enforced. Grown-up people had good manners, and wished to see them reflected in the young. Nowadays, the imitation is always voluntary. Grown-up people have no manners at all; whereas they certainly have a very keen taste for the intrinsic charm of children. They wish children to be perfectly natural. That is (aesthetically at least) an admirable wish. My complaint against these grown-up people is, that they themselves, whom time has robbed of their natural grace as surely as it robs the other animals, are content to be perfectly natural. This contentment I deplore, and am keen to disturb.

I except from my indictment any young lady who may read these words. I will assume that she differs from the rest of the human race, and has not, never had, anything to learn in the art of conversing prettily, of entering or leaving a room or a vehicle gracefully, of writing appropriate letters, et patati et patata. I will assume that all these accomplishments came naturally to her. She will now be in a mood to accept my proposition that of her contemporaries none seems to have been so lucky as herself. She will agree with me that other girls need training. She will not deny that grace in the little affairs of life is a thing which has to be learned. Some girls have a far greater aptitude for learning it than others; but, with one exception, no girls have it in them from the outset. It is a not less complicated thing than is the art of acting, or of nursing the sick, and needs for the acquirement of it a not less laborious preparation.

Is it worth the trouble? Certainly the trouble is not taken. The 'finishing school,' wherein young ladies were taught to be graceful, is a thing of the past. It must have been a dismal place; but the dismalness of it—the strain of it—was the measure of its indispensability. There I beg the question. Is grace itself indispensable? Certainly, it has been dispensed with. It isn't reckoned with. To sit perfectly mute 'in company,' or to chatter on at the top of one's voice; to shriek with laughter; to fling oneself into a room and dash oneself out of it; to collapse on chairs or sofas; to sprawl across tables; to slam doors; to write, without punctuation, notes that only an expert in handwriting could read, and only an expert in mis-spelling could understand;

to hustle, to bounce, to go straight ahead—to be, let us say, perfectly natural in the midst of an artificial civilisation, is an ideal which the young ladies of to-day are neither publicly nor privately discouraged from cherishing. The word 'cherishing' implies a softness of which they are not guilty. I hasten to substitute 'pursuing.' If these young ladies were not in the aforesaid midst of an artificial civilisation, I should be the last to discourage their pursuit. If they were Amazons, for example, spending their lives beneath the sky, in tilth of stubborn fields, and in armed conflict with fierce men, it would be unreasonable to expect of them any sacrifice to the Graces. But they are exposed to no such hardships. They have a really very comfortable sort of life. They are not expected to be useful. (I am writing all the time, of course, about the young ladies in the affluent classes.) And it seems to me that they, in payment of their debt to Fate, ought to occupy the time that is on their hands by becoming ornamental, and increasing the world's store of beauty. In a sense, certainly, they are ornamental. It is a strange fact, and an ironic, that they spend quite five times the annual amount that was spent by their grandmothers on personal adornment. If they can afford it, well and good: let us have no sumptuary law. But plenty of pretty dresses will not suffice. Pretty manners are needed with them, and are prettier than they.

I had forgotten men. Every defect that I had noted in the modern young woman is not less notable in the modern young man. Briefly, he is a boor. If it is true that 'manners makyth man,' one doubts whether the British race can be perpetuated. The young Englishman of to-day is inferior to savages and to beasts of the field in that they are eager to show themselves in an agreeable and seductive light to the females of their kind, whilst he regards any such effort as beneath his dignity. Not that he cultivates dignity in demeanour. He merely slouches. Unlike his feminine counterpart, he lets his raiment match his manners. Observe him any afternoon, as he passes down Piccadilly, sullenly, with his shoulders humped, and his hat clapped to the back of his head, and his cigarette dangling almost vertically from his lips. It seems only appropriate that his hat is a billy-cock, and his shirt a flannel one, and that his boots are brown ones. Thus attired, he is on his way to pay a visit of ceremony to some house at which he has recently dined. No; that is the sort of visit he never pays. (I must confess I don't myself.) But one remembers the time when no self-respecting youth would have shown himself in Piccadilly without the vesture appropriate to that august highway. Nowadays there is no care for appearances. Comfort is the one aim. Any care for appearances is regarded rather as a sign of effeminacy. Yet never, in any other age of the world's history, has it been regarded so. Indeed, elaborate dressing used to be deemed by philosophers an outcome of the sex-instinct. It was supposed that men dressed themselves finely in order to attract the admiration of women, just as peacocks spread their plumage with a similar purpose. Nor do I jettison the old theory. The declension of masculine attire in England began soon after the time when statistics were beginning to show the great numerical preponderance of women over men; and is it fanciful to trace the one fact to the other? Surely not. I do not say that either sex is attracted to the other by elaborate attire. But I believe that each sex, consciously or unconsciously, uses this elaboration for this very purpose. Thus the over-dressed girl of to-day and the ill-dressed youth are but symbols of the balance of our population. The one is pleading, the other scorning. 'Take me!' is the message borne by the furs and the pearls and the old lace. 'I'll see about that when I've had a look round!' is the not pretty answer conveyed by the billy-cock and the flannel shirt.

I dare say that fine manners, like fine clothes, are one of the stratagems of sex. This theory squares at once with the modern young man's lack of manners. But how about the modern young woman's not less obvious lack? Well, the theory will square with that, too. The modern young woman's gracelessness may be due to her conviction that men like a girl to be thoroughly natural. She knows that they have a very high opinion of themselves; and what, thinks she, more natural than that they should esteem her in proportion to her power of reproducing the qualities that are most salient in themselves? Men, she perceives, are clumsy, and talk loud, and have no drawing-room accomplishments, and are rude; and she proceeds to model herself on them. Let us not blame her. Let us blame rather her parents or guardians, who, though they well know that a masculine girl attracts no man, leave her to the devices of her own inexperience. Girls ought not to be allowed, as they are, to run wild. So soon as they have lost the natural grace of childhood, they should be initiated into that course of artificial training through which their grandmothers passed before them, and in virtue of which their grandmothers were pleasing. This will not, of course, ensure husbands for them all; but it will certainly tend to increase the number of marriages. Nor is it primarily for that sociological reason that I plead for a return to the old system of education. I plead for it, first and last, on aesthetic grounds. Let the Graces be cultivated for their own sweet sake.

The difficulty is how to begin. The mothers of the rising generation were brought up in the unregenerate way. Their scraps of oral tradition will need to be supplemented by much research. I advise them to start their quest by reading The Young Lady's Book. Exactly the right spirit is therein enshrined, though of the substance there is much that could not be well applied to our own day. That chapter on 'The Escrutoire,' for example, belongs to a day that cannot be recalled. We can get rid of bad manners, but we cannot substitute the Sedan-chair for the motor-car; and the penny post, with telephones and telegrams, has, in our own beautiful phrase, 'come to stay,' and has elbowed the art of letter-writing irrevocably from among us. But notes are still written; and there is no reason why they should not be written well. Has the mantle of those anonymous gentlewomen who wrote The Young Lady's Book fallen on no one? Will no one revise that 'Manual of Elegant Recreations, Exercises, and Pursuits,' adapting it to present needs?... A few hints as to Deportment in the Motor-Car; the exact Angle whereat to hold the Receiver of a Telephone, and the exact Key wherein to pitch the Voice; the Conduct of a Cigarette... I see a wide and golden vista.

WHISTLER'S WRITING

No book-lover, I. Give me an uninterrupted view of my fellow-creatures. The most tedious of them pleases me better than the best book. You see, I admit that some of them are tedious. I do not deem alien from myself nothing that is human: I discriminate my fellow-creatures according to their contents. And in that respect I am not more different in my way from the true humanitarian than from the true bibliophile in his. To him the content of a book matters not at all. He loves books because they are books, and discriminates them only by the irrelevant standard of their rarity. A rare book is not less dear to him because it is unreadable, even as to the snob a dull duke is as good as a bright one. Indeed, why should he bother about readableness? He doesn't want to read. 'Uncut edges' for him, when he can get them; and, even when he can't, the notion of reading a rare edition would seem to him quite uncouth and preposterous The aforesaid snob would as soon question His Grace about the state of His Grace's soul. I, on the other hand, whenever human company is denied me, have often a desire to read. Reading, I prefer cut edges, because a paper-knife is one of the things that have the gift of invisibility whenever they are wanted; and because one's thumb, in prising open the pages, so often affects the text. Many volumes have I thus mutilated, and I hope that in the sale-rooms of a sentimental posterity they may fetch higher prices than their duly uncut duplicates. So long as my thumb tatters merely the margin, I am quite equanimous. If I were reading a First Folio Shakespeare by my fireside, and if the matchbox were ever so little beyond my reach, I vow I would light my cigarette with a spill made from the margin of whatever page I were reading. I am neat, scrupulously neat, in regard to the things I care about; but a book, as a book, is not one of these things.

Of course, a book may happen to be in itself a beautiful object. Such a book I treat tenderly, as one would a flower. And such a book is, in its brown-papered boards, whereon gleam little gilt italics and a little gilt butterfly, Whistler's Gentle Art of Making Enemies. It happens to be also a book which I have read again and again—a book that has often travelled with me. Yet its cover is as fresh as when first, some twelve years since, it came into my possession. A flower freshly plucked, one would say—a brown-and-yellow flower, with a little gilt butterfly fluttering over it. And its inner petals, its delicately proportioned pages, are as white and undishevelled as though they never had been opened. The book lies open before me, as I write. I must be careful of my pen's transit from inkpot to MS.

Yet, I know, many worthy folk would like the book blotted out of existence. These are they who understand and love the art of painting, but neither love nor understand writing as an art. For them The Gentle Art of Making

Enemies is but something unworthy of a great man. Certainly, it is a thing incongruous with a great hero. And for most people it is painful not to regard a great man as also a great hero; hence all the efforts to explain away the moral characteristics deducible from The Gentle Art of Making Enemies, and to prove that Whistler, beneath a prickly surface, was saturated through and through with the quintessence of the Sermon on the Mount.

Well! hero-worship is a very good thing. It is a wholesome exercise which we ought all to take, now and again. Only, let us not strain ourselves by overdoing it. Let us not indulge in it too constantly. Let hero-worship be reserved for heroes. And there was nothing heroic about Whistler, except his unfaltering devotion to his own ideals in art. No saint was he, and none would have been more annoyed than he by canonisation; would he were here to play, as he would have played incomparably, the devil's advocate! So far as he possessed the Christian virtues, his faith was in himself, his hope was for the immortality of his own works, and his charity was for the defects in those works. He is known to have been an affectionate son, an affectionate husband; but, for the rest, all the tenderness in him seems to have been absorbed into his love for such things in nature as were expressible through terms of his own art. As a man in relation to his fellow-men, he cannot, from any purely Christian standpoint, be applauded. He was inordinately vain and cantankerous. Enemies, as he has wittily implied, were a necessity to his nature; and he seems to have valued friendship (a thing never really valuable, in itself, to a really vain man) as just the needful foundation for future enmity. Quarrelling and picking quarrels, he went his way through life blithely. Most of these quarrels were quite trivial and tedious. In the ordinary way, they would have been forgotten long ago, as the trivial and tedious details in the lives of other great men are forgotten. But Whistler was great not merely in painting, not merely as a wit and dandy in social life. He had, also, an extraordinary talent for writing. He was a born writer. He wrote, in his way, perfectly; and his way was his own, and the secret of it has died with him. Thus, conducting them through the Post Office, he has conducted his squabbles to immortality.

Immortality is a big word. I do not mean by it that so long as this globe shall endure, the majority of the crawlers round it will spend the greater part of their time in reading The Gentle Art of Making Enemies. Even the pre-eminently immortal works of Shakespeare are read very little. The average of time devoted to them by Englishmen cannot (even though one assess Mr. Frank Harris at eight hours per diem, and Mr. Sidney Lee at twenty-four) tot up to more than a small fraction of a second in a lifetime reckoned by the Psalmist's limit. When I dub Whistler an immortal writer, I do but mean that so long as there are a few people interested in the subtler ramifications of

English prose as an art-form, so long will there be a few constantly-recurring readers of The Gentle Art.

There are in England, at this moment, a few people to whom prose appeals as an art; but none of them, I think, has yet done justice to Whistler's prose. None has taken it with the seriousness it deserves. I am not surprised. When a man can express himself through two media, people tend to take him lightly in his use of the medium to which he devotes the lesser time and energy, even though he use that medium not less admirably than the other, and even though they themselves care about it more than they care about the other. Perhaps this very preference in them creates a prejudice against the man who does not share it, and so makes them sceptical of his power. Anyhow, if Disraeli had been unable to express himself through the medium of political life, Disraeli's novels would long ago have had the due which the expert is just beginning to give them. Had Rossetti not been primarily a poet, the expert in painting would have acquired long ago his present penetration into the peculiar value of Rossetti's painting. Likewise, if Whistler had never painted a picture, and, even so, had written no more than he actually did write, this essay in appreciation would have been forestalled again and again. As it is, I am a sort of herald. And, however loudly I shall blow my trumpet, not many people will believe my message. For many years to come, it will be the fashion among literary critics to pooh-pooh Whistler, the writer, as an amateur. For Whistler was primarily a painter—not less than was Rossetti primarily a poet, and Disraeli a statesman. And he will not live down quicklier than they the taunt of amateurishness in his secondary art. Nevertheless, I will, for my own pleasure, blow the trumpet.

I grant you, Whistler was an amateur. But you do not dispose of a man by proving him to be an amateur. On the contrary, an amateur with real innate talent may do, must do, more exquisite work than he could do if he were a professional. His very ignorance and tentativeness may be, must be, a means of especial grace. Not knowing 'how to do things,' having no ready-made and ready-working apparatus, and being in constant fear of failure, he has to grope always in the recesses of his own soul for the best way to express his soul's meaning. He has to shift for himself, and to do his very best. Consequently, his work has a more personal and fresher quality, and a more exquisite 'finish,' than that of a professional, howsoever finely endowed. All of the much that we admire in Walter Pater's prose comes of the lucky chance that he was an amateur, and never knew his business. Had Fate thrown him out of Oxford upon the world, the world would have been the richer for the prose of another John Addington Symonds, and would have forfeited Walter Pater's prose. In other words, we should have lost a half-crown and found a shilling. Had Fate withdrawn from Whistler his vision for form and colour, leaving him only his taste for words and phrases and cadences, Whistler would have settled solidly down to the art of writing, and would have mastered it, and, mastering it, have lost that especial quality which the Muse grants only to them who approach her timidly, bashfully, as suitors.

Perhaps I am wrong. Perhaps Whistler would never, in any case, have acquired the professional touch in writing. For we know that he never acquired it in the art to which he dedicated all but the surplus of his energy. Compare him with the other painters of his day. He was a child in comparison with them. They, with sure science, solved roughly and readily problems of modelling and drawing and what not that he never dared to meddle with. It has often been said that his art was an art of evasion. But the reason of the evasion was reverence. He kept himself reverently at a distance. He knew how much he could not do, nor was he ever confident even of the things that he could do; and these things, therefore, he did superlatively well, having to grope for the means in the recesses of his soul. The particular quality of exquisiteness and freshness that gives to all his work, whether on canvas or on stone or on copper, a distinction from and above any contemporary work, and makes it dearer to our eyes and hearts, is a quality that came to him because he was an amateur, and that abided with him because he never ceased to be an amateur. He was a master through his lack of mastery. In the art of writing, too, he was a master through his lack of mastery. There is an almost exact parallel between the two sides of his genius. Nothing could be more absurd than the general view of him as a masterly professional on the one side and a trifling amateur on the other. He was, certainly, a painter who wrote; but, by the slightest movement of Fate's little finger, he might have been a writer who painted, and this essay have been written not by me from my standpoint, but by some painter, eager to suggest that Whistler's painting was a quite serious thing.

Yes, that painting and that writing are marvellously akin; and such differences as you will see in them are superficial merely. I spoke of Whistler's vanity in life, and I spoke of his timidity and reverence in art. That contradiction is itself merely superficial. Bob Acres was timid, but he was also vain. His swagger was not an empty assumption to cloak his fears; he really did regard himself as a masterful and dare-devil fellow, except when he was actually fighting. Similarly, except when he was at his work, Whistler, doubtless, really did think of himself as a brilliant effortless butterfly. The pose was, doubtless a quite sincere one, a necessary reaction of feeling. Well, in his writing he displays to us his vanity; whilst in his Painting we discern only his reverence. In his writing, too, he displays his harshness—swoops hither and thither a butterfly equipped with sharp little beak and talons; whereas in his painting we are conscious only of his caressing sense of beauty. But look from the writer, as shown by himself, to the means by which himself is shown. You will find that for words as for colour-tones he has the same reverent care, and for phrases as for forms the same caressing sense of beauty. Fastidiousness—'daintiness,' as he would have said—dandyishness, as we might well say: by just that which marks him as a painter is he marked as a writer too. His meaning was ever ferocious; but his method, how delicate and tender! The portrait of his mother, whom he loved, was not wrought with a more loving hand than were his portraits of Mr. Harry Quilter for The World.

His style never falters. The silhouette of no sentence is ever blurred. Every sentence is ringing with a clear vocal cadence. There, after all, in that vocal quality, is the chief test of good writing. Writing, as a means of expression, has to compete with talking. The talker need not rely wholly on what he says. He has the help of his mobile face and hands, and of his voice, with its various inflexions and its variable pace, whereby he may insinuate fine shades of meaning, qualifying or strengthening at will, and clothing naked words with colour, and making dead words live. But the writer? He can express a certain amount through his handwriting, if he write in a properly elastic way. But his writing is not printed in facsimile. It is printed in cold, mechanical, monotonous type. For his every effect he must rely wholly on the words that he chooses, and on the order in which he ranges them, and on his choice among the few hard-and-fast symbols of punctuation. He must so use those slender means that they shall express all that he himself can express through his voice and face and hands, or all that he would thus express if he were a good talker. Usually, the good talker is a dead failure when he tries to express himself in writing. For that matter, so is the bad talker. But the bad talker has the better chance of success, inasmuch as the inexpressiveness of his voice and face and hands will have sharpened his scent for words and phrases that shall in themselves convey such meanings as he has to express. Whistler was that rare phenomenon, the good talker who could write as well as he talked. Read any page of The Gentle Art of Making Enemies, and you will hear a voice in it, and see a face in it, and see gestures in it. And none of these is quite like any other known to you. It matters not that you never knew Whistler, never even set eyes on him. You see him and know him here. The voice drawls slowly, quickening to a kind of snap at the end of every sentence, and sometimes rising to a sudden screech of laughter; and, all the while, the fine fierce eyes of the talker are flashing out at you, and his long nervous fingers are tracing extravagant arabesques in the air. No! you need never have seen Whistler to know what he was like. He projected through printed words the clean-cut image and clear-ringing echo of himself. He was a born writer, achieving perfection through pains which must have been infinite for that we see at first sight no trace of them at all.

Like himself, necessarily, his style was cosmopolitan and eccentric. It comprised Americanisms and Cockneyisms and Parisian argot, with constant reminiscences of the authorised version of the Old Testament, and with chips off Molie're, and with shreds and tags of what-not snatched from a hundred-and-one queer corners. It was, in fact, an Autolycine style. It was a style of the maddest motley, but of motley so deftly cut and fitted to the figure, and worn with such an air, as to become a gracious harmony for all beholders.

After all, what matters is not so much the vocabulary as the manner in which the vocabulary is used. Whistler never failed to find right words, and the right cadence for a dignified meaning, when dignity was his aim. 'And when the evening mist clothes the riverside with poetry, as with a veil, and the poor buildings lose themselves in the dim sky, and the tall chimneys become campanili, and the warehouses are palaces in the night, and the whole city hangs in the heavens, and fairyland is before us...' That is as perfect, in its dim and delicate beauty, as any of his painted 'nocturnes.' But his aim was more often to pour ridicule and contempt. And herein the weirdness of his natural vocabulary and the patchiness of his reading were of very real value to him. Take the opening words of his letter to Tom Taylor: 'Dead for a ducat, dead! my dear Tom: and the rattle has reached me by post. Sans rancune, say you? Bah! you scream unkind threats and die badly...' And another letter to the same unfortunate man: 'Why, my dear old Tom, I never was serious with you, even when you were among us. Indeed, I killed you quite, as who should say, without seriousness, "A rat! A rat!" you know, rather cursorily...' There the very lack of coherence in the style, as of a man gasping and choking with laughter, drives the insults home with a horrible precision. Notice the technical skill in the placing of 'you know, rather cursorily' at the end of the sentence. Whistler was full of such tricks—tricks that could never have been played by him, could never have occurred to him, had he acquired the professional touch And not a letter in the book but has some such little sharp felicity of cadence or construction.

The letters, of course, are the best thing in the book, and the best of the letters are the briefest. An exquisite talent like Whistler's, whether in painting or in writing, is always at its best on a small scale. On a large scale it strays and is distressed. Thus the 'Ten o'Clock,' from which I took that passage about the evening mist and the riverside, does not leave me with a sense of artistic satisfaction. It lacks structure. It is not a roundly conceived whole: it is but a row of fragments. Were it otherwise, Whistler could never have written so perfectly the little letters. For no man who can finely grasp a big theme can play exquisitely round a little one.

Nor can any man who excels in scoffing at his fellows excel also in taking abstract subjects seriously. Certainly, the little letters are Whistler's passport among the elect of literature. Luckily, I can judge them without prejudice. Whether in this or that case Whistler was in the right or in the wrong is not a question which troubles me at all. I read the letters simply from the literary standpoint. As controversial essays, certainly, they were often in very bad taste. An urchin scribbling insults upon somebody's garden-wall would not go further than Whistler often went. Whistler's mode of controversy reminds me, in another sense, of the writing on the wall. They who were so foolish as to oppose him really did have their souls required of them. After an encounter with him they never again were quite the same men in the eyes of their fellows. Whistler's insults always stuck—stuck and spread round the insulted, who found themselves at length encased in them, like flies in amber.

You may shed a tear over the flies, if you will. For myself, I am content to laud the amber.

ICHABOD

It is not cast from any obvious mould of sentiment. It is not a memorial urn, nor a ruined tower, nor any of those things which he who runs may weep over. Though not less really deplorable than they, it needs, I am well aware, some sort of explanation to enable my reader to mourn with me. For it is merely a hat-box.

It is nothing but that—an ordinary affair of pig-skin, with a brass lock. As I write, it stands on a table near me. It is of the kind that accommodates two hats, one above the other. It has had many tenants, and is sun-tanned, rain-soiled, scarred and dented by collision with trucks and what not other accessories to the moving scenes through which it has been bandied. Yes! it has known the stress of many journeys; yet has it never (you would say, seeing it) received its baptism of paste: it has not one label on it. And there, indeed, is the tragedy that I shall unfold.

For many years this hat-box had been my travelling companion, and was, but a few days since, a dear record of all the big and little journeys I had made. It was much more to me than a mere receptacle for hats. It was my one collection, my collection of labels. Well! last week its lock was broken. I sent it to the trunk-makers, telling them to take the greatest care of it. It came back yesterday. The idiots, the accursed idots! had carefully removed every label from its surface. I wrote to them—it matters not what I said. My fury has burnt itself out. I have reached the stage of craving general sympathy. So I have sat down to write, in the shadow of a tower which stands bleak, bare, prosaic, all the ivy of its years stripped from it; in the shadow of an urn commemorating nothing.

I think that every one who is or ever has been a collector will pity me in this dark hour of mine. In other words, I think that nearly every one will pity me. For few are they who have not, at some time, come under the spell of the collecting spirit and known the joy of accumulating specimens of something or other. The instinct has its corner, surely, in every breast. Of course, hobby-horses are of many different breeds; but all their riders belong to one great cavalcade, and when they know that one of their company has had his steed shot under him, they will not ride on without a backward glance of sympathy. Lest my fall be unnoted by them, I write this essay. I want that glance.

Do not, reader, suspect that because I am choosing my words nicely, and playing with metaphor, and putting my commas in their proper places, my sorrow is not really and truly poignant. I write elaborately, for that is my habit, and habits are less easily broken than hearts. I could no more 'dash off' this my cri de coeur than I could an elegy on a broomstick I had never seen. Therefore, reader, bear with me, despite my sable plumes and purple; and weep with me, though my prose be, like those verses which Mr. Beamish wrote over Chloe's grave, 'of a character to cool emotion.' For indeed my anguish is very real. The collection I had amassed so carefully, during so many years, the collection I loved and revelled in, has been obliterated, swept away, destroyed utterly by a pair of ruthless, impious, well-meaning, idiotic, unseen hands. It cannot be restored to me. Nothing can compensate me for it gone. It was part and parcel of my life.

Orchids, jade, majolica, wines, mezzotints, old silver, first editions, harps, copes, hookahs, cameos, enamels, black-letter folios, scarabaei—such things are beautiful and fascinating in themselves. Railway-labels are not, I admit. For the most part, they are crudely coloured, crudely printed, without sense of margin or spacing; in fact, quite worthless as designs. No one would be a connoisseur in them. No one could be tempted to make a general collection of them. My own collection of them was strictly personal: I wanted none that was not a symbol of some journey made by myself, even as the hunter of big game cares not to possess the tusks, and the hunter of women covets not the photographs, of other people's victims. My collection was one of those which result from man's tendency to preserve some obvious record of his pleasures—the points he has scored in the game. To Nimrod, his tusks; to Lothario, his photographs; to me (who cut no dash in either of those veneries, and am not greedy enough to preserve menus nor silly enough to preserve press-cuttings, but do delight in travelling from place to place), my railway-labels. Had nomady been my business, had I been a commercial traveller or a King's Messenger, such labels would have held for me no charming significance. But I am only by instinct a nomad. I have a tether, known as the four-mile radius. To slip it is for me always an event, an excitement. To come to a new place, to awaken in a strange bed, to be among strangers! To have dispelled, as by sudden magic, the old environment! It is on the scoring of such points as these that I preen myself, and my memory is always ringing the 'changes' I have had, complacently, as a man jingles silver in his pocket. The noise of a great terminus is no jar to me. It is music. I prick up my ears to it, and paw the platform. Dear to me as the bugle-note to any war-horse, as the first twittering of the birds in the hedgerows to the light-sleeping vagabond, that cry of 'Take your seats please!' or—better still—'En voiture!' or 'Partenza!' Had I the knack of rhyme, I would write a sonnet-sequence of the journey to Newhaven or Dover—a sonnet for every station one does not stop at. I await that poet who shall worthily celebrate the iron road. There is one who describes, with accuracy and gusto, the insides of engines; but he will not do at all. I look for another, who shall show us the heart of the passenger, the exhilaration of travelling by day, the exhilaration and romance and self-importance of travelling by night.

'Paris!' How it thrills me when, on a night in spring, in the hustle and glare of Victoria, that label is slapped upon my hat-box! Here, standing in the very heart of London, I am by one sweep of a paste-brush transported instantly into that white-grey city across the sea. To all intents and purposes I am in Paris already. Strange, that the porter does not say, 'V'la', M'sieu'!' Strange, that the evening papers I buy at the bookstall are printed in the English language. Strange, that London still holds my body, when a corduroyed magician has whisked my soul verily into Paris. The engine is hissing as I hurry my body along the platform, eager to reunite it with my soul... Over the windy quay the stars are shining as I pass down the gangway, hat-box in hand. They twinkle brightly over the deck I am now pacing—amused, may be, at my excitement. The machinery grunts and creaks. The little boat quakes in the excruciating throes of its departure. At last!... One by one, the stars take their last look at me, and the sky grows pale, and the sea blanches mysteriously with it. Through the delicate cold air of the dawn, across the grey waves of the sea, the outlines of Dieppe grow and grow. The quay is lined with its blue-bloused throng. These porters are as excited by us as though they were the aborigines of some unknown island. (And yet, are they not here, at this hour, in these circumstances, every day of their lives?) These gestures! These voices, hoarse with passion! The dear music of French, rippling up clear for me through all this hoarse confusion of its utterance, and making me happy!... I drink my cup of steaming coffee—true coffee!—and devour more than one roll. At the tables around me, pale and dishevelled from the night, sit the people whom I saw—years ago!—at Charing Cross. How they have changed! The coffee sends a glow throughout my body. I am fulfilled with a sense of material well-being. The queer ethereal exaltation of the dawn has vanished. I climb up into the train, and dispose myself in the dun-cushioned coupé. 'Chemins de Fer de l'Ouest' is perforated on the white antimacassars. Familiar and strange inscription! I murmur its impressive iambs over and over again. They become the refrain to which the train vibrates on its way. I smoke cigarettes, a little drowsily gazing out of the window at the undulating French scenery that flies past me, at the silver poplars. Row after slanted row of these incomparably gracious trees flies past me, their foliage shimmering in the unawoken landscape Soon I shall be rattling over the cobbles of unawoken Paris, through the wide white-grey streets with their unopened jalousies. And when, later, I awake in the unnatural little bedroom of walnut-wood and crimson velvet, in the bed whose curtains are white with that whiteness which Paris alone can give to linen, a Parisian sun will be glittering for me in a Parisian sky.

Yes! In my whole collection the Paris specimens were dearest to me, meant most to me, I think. But there was none that had not some tendrils on sentiment. All of them I prized, more or less. Of the Aberdeen specimens I was immensely fond. Who can resist the thought of that express by which, night after night, England is torn up its centre? I love well that cab-drive in the chill autumnal night through the desert of Bloomsbury, the dead leaves rustling round the horse's hoofs as we gallop through the Squares. Ah, I shall be across the Border before these doorsteps are cleaned, before the coming of the milk-carts. Anon, I descry the cavernous open jaws of Euston. The monster swallows me, and soon I am being digested into Scotland. I sit ensconced in a corner of a compartment. The collar of my ulster is above my ears, my cap is pulled over my eyes, my feet are on a hot-water tin, and my rug snugly envelops most of me. Sleeping-cars are for the strange beings who love not the act of travelling. Them I should spurn even if I could not sleep a wink in an ordinary compartment. I would liefer forfeit sleep than the consciousness of travelling. But it happens that I, in an ordinary compartment, am blest both with the sleep and with the consciousness, all through the long night. To be asleep and to know that you are sleeping, and to know, too, that even as you sleep you are being borne away through darkness into distance—that, surely, is to go two better than Endymion. Surely, nothing is more mysteriously delightful than this joint consciousness of sleep and movement. Pitiable they to whom it is denied. All through the night the vibration of the train keeps one-third of me awake, while the other two parts of me profoundly slumber. Whenever the train stops, and the vibration ceases, then the one-third of me falls asleep, and the other two parts stir. I am awake just enough to hear the hollow-echoing cry of 'Crewe' or 'York,' and to blink up at the green-hooded lamp in the ceiling. May be, I raise a corner of the blind, and see through the steam-dim window the mysterious, empty station. A solitary porter shuffles along the platform. Yonder, those are the lights of the refreshment room, where, all night long, a barmaid is keeping her lonely vigil over the beer-handles and the Bath-buns in glass cases. I see long rows of glimmering milk-cans, and wonder drowsily whether they contain forty modern thieves. The engine snorts angrily in the benighted silence. Far away is the faint, familiar sound—clink-clank, clink-clank—of the man who tests the couplings. Nearer and nearer the sound comes. It passes, recedes It is rather melancholy.... A whistle, a jerk, and the two waking parts of me are asleep again, while the third wakes up to mount guard over them, and keeps me deliciously aware of the rhythmic dream they are dreaming about the hot bath and the clean linen, and the lovely breakfast that I am to have at Aberdeen; and of the Scotch air, crisp and keen, that is to escort me, later along the Deeside.

Little journeys, as along the Deeside, have a charm of their own. Little journeys from London to places up the river, or to places on the coast of Kent—journeys so brief that you lunch at one end and have tea at the other—I love them all, and loved the labels that recalled them to me. But the labels of long journeys, of course, took precedence in my heart. Here and there on my hat-box were labels that recalled to me long journeys in which frontiers were crossed at dead of night—dim memories of small, crazy stations where I shivered half-awake, and was sleepily conscious of a strange tongue and strange uniforms, of my jingling bunch of keys, of ruthless arms diving into the nethermost recesses of my trunks, of suspicious grunts and glances, and of grudging hieroglyphics chalked on the slammed lids. These were things more or less painful and resented in the moment of experience, yet even then fraught with a delicious glamour. I suffered, but gladly. In the night, when all things are mysteriously magnified, I have never crossed a frontier without feeling some of the pride of conquest. And, indeed, were these conquests mere illusions? Was I not actually extending the frontiers of my mind, adding new territories to it? Every crossed frontier, every crossed sea, meant for me a definite success—an expansion and enrichment of my soul. When, after seven days and nights of sea traversed, I caught my first glimpse of Sandy Hook, was there no comparison between Columbus and myself? To see what one has not seen before, is not that almost as good as to see what no one has ever seen?

Romance, exhilaration, self-importance these are what my labels symbolised and recalled to me. That lost collection was a running record of all my happiest hours; a focus, a monument, a diary. It was my humble Odyssey, wrought in coloured paper on pig-skin, and the one work I never, never was weary of. If the distinguished Ithacan had travelled with a hat-box, how finely and minutely Homer would have described it—its depth and girth, its cunningly fashioned lock and fair lining withal! And in how interminable a torrent of hexameters would he have catalogued all the labels on it, including those attractive views of the Hotel Circe, the Hotel Calypso, and other high-class resorts. Yet no! Had such a hat-box existed and had it been preserved in his day, Homer would have seen in it a sufficient record, a better record than even he could make, of Odysseus' wanderings. We should have had nothing from him but the Iliad. I, certainly never felt any need of commemorating my journeys till my labels were lost to me. And I am conscious how poor and chill is the substitute.

My collection like most collections, began imperceptibly. A man does not say to himself, 'I am going to collect' this thing or that. True, the schoolboy says so; but his are not, in the true sense of the word, collections. He seeks no set autobiographic symbols, for boys never look back—there is too little to look back on, too much in front. Nor have the objects of his collection any intrinsic charm for him. He starts a collection merely that he may have a plausible excuse for doing something he ought not to do. He goes in for birds' eggs merely that he may be allowed to risk his bones and tear his clothes in climbing; for butterflies, that he may be encouraged to poison and impale; for stamps...really, I do not know why he, why any sane creature goes in for stamps. It follows that he has no real love of his collection and soon abandons it for something else. The sincere collector, how different! His hobby has a solid basis of personal preference. Some one gives him (say) a piece of jade. He admires it. He sees another piece in a shop, and buys it; later, he buys another. He does not regard these pieces of jade as distinct from the rest of his possessions; he has no idea of collecting jade. It is not till he has acquired several other pieces that he ceases to regard them as mere items in the decoration of his room, and gives them a little table, or a tray of a cabinet, all to themselves. How well they look there! How they intensify one another! He really must get some one to give him that little pedestalled Cupid which he saw yesterday in Wardour Street. Thus awakes in him, quite gradually, the spirit of the collector. Or take the case of one whose collection is not of beautiful things, but of autobiographic symbols: take the case of the glutton. He will have pocketed many menus before it occurs to him to arrange them in an album. Even so, it was not until a fair number of labels had been pasted on my hat-box that I saw them as souvenirs, and determined that in future my hat-box should always travel with me and so commemorate my every darling escape.

In the path of every collector are strewn obstacles of one kind or another; which, to overleap, is part of the fun. As a collector of labels I had my pleasant difficulties. On any much-belabelled piece of baggage the porter always pastes the new label over that which looks most recent; else the thing might miss its destination. Now, paste dries before the end of the briefest journey; and one of my canons was that, though two labels might overlap, none must efface the inscription of another. On the other hand, I did not wish to lose my hat-box, for this would have entailed inquiries, and descriptions, and telegraphing up the line, and all manner of agitation. What, then, was I to do? I might have taken my hat-box with me in the carriage? That, indeed, is what I always did. But, unless a thing is to go in the van, it receives no label at all. So I had to use a mild stratagem. 'Yes,' I would say, 'everything in the van!' The labels would be duly affixed. 'Oh,' I would cry, seizing the hat-box quickly, 'I forgot. I want this with me in the carriage.' (I learned to seize it quickly, because some porters are such martinets that they will whisk the label off and confiscate it.) Then, when the man was not looking, I would remove the label from the place he had chosen for it and press it on some unoccupied part of the surface. You cannot think how much I enjoyed these manoeuvres. There was the moral pleasure of having both outwitted a railway company and secured another specimen for my collection; and there was the physical pleasure of making a limp slip of paper stick to a hard substance—that simple pleasure which appeals to all of us and is, perhaps, the missing explanation of philately. Pressed for time, I could not, of course, have played my trick. Nor could I have done so—it would have seemed heartless—if any one had come to see me off and be agitated at parting. Therefore, I was always very careful to arrive in good time for my train, and to insist that all farewells should be made on my own doorstep.

Only in one case did I break the rule that no label must be obliterated by another. It is a long story; but I propose to tell it. You must know that I loved my labels not only for the meanings they conveyed to me, but also, more than a little, for the effect they produced on other people. Travelling in a compartment, with my hat-box beside me, I enjoyed the silent interest which my labels aroused in my fellow-passengers. If the compartment was so full that my hat-box had to be relegated to the rack, I would always, in the course of the journey, take it down and unlock it, and pretend to be looking for something I had put into it. It pleased me to see from beneath my eyelids the respectful wonder and envy evoked by it. Of course, there was no suspicion that the labels were a carefully formed collection; they were taken as the wild-flowers of an exquisite restlessness, of an unrestricted range in life. Many of them signified beautiful or famous places. There was one point at which Oxford, Newmarket, and Assisi converged, and I was always careful to shift my hat-box round in such a way that this purple patch should be lost on none of my fellow-passengers. The many other labels, English or alien, they, too, gave their hints of a life spent in fastidious freedom, hints that I had seen and was seeing all that is best to be seen of men and cities and country-houses. I was respected, accordingly, and envied. And I had keen delight in this ill-gotten homage. A despicable delight, you say? But is not yours, too, a fallen nature? The love of impressing strangers falsely, is it not implanted in all of us? To be sure, it is an inevitable outcome of the conditions in which we exist. It is a result of the struggle for life. Happiness, as you know, is our aim in life; we are all struggling to be happy. And, alas! for every one of us, it is the things he does not possess which seem to him most desirable, most conducive to happiness. For instance, the poor nobleman covets wealth, because wealth would bring him comfort, whereas the nouveau riche covets a pedigree, because a pedigree would make him of what he is merely in. The rich nobleman who is an invalid covets health, on the assumption that health would enable him to enjoy his wealth and position. The rich, robust nobleman hankers after an intellect. The rich, robust, intellectual nobleman is (be sure of it) as discontented, somehow, as the rest of them. No man possesses all he wants. No man is ever quite happy. But, by producing an impression that he has what he wants—in fact, by 'bluffing'—a man can gain some of the advantages that he would gain by really having it. Thus, the poor nobleman can, by concealing his 'balance' and keeping up appearances, coax more or less unlimited credit from his tradesman. The nouveau riche, by concealing his origin and trafficking with the College of Heralds, can intercept some of the homage paid to high birth. And (though the rich nobleman who is an invalid can make no tangible gain by pretending to be robust, since robustness is an advantage only from within) the rich, robust nobleman can, by employing a clever private secretary to write public speeches and magazine articles for him, intercept some of the homage which is paid to intellect.

These are but a few typical cases, taken at random from a small area. But consider the human race at large, and you will find that 'bluffing' is indeed one of the natural functions of the human animal. Every man pretends to have what (not having it) he covets, in order that he may gain some of the advantages of having it. And thus it comes that he makes his pretence, also, by force of habit, when there is nothing tangible to be gained by it. The poor nobleman wishes to be thought rich even by people who will not benefit him in their delusion; and the nouveau riche likes to be thought well-born even by people who set no store on good birth; and so forth. But pretences, whether they be an end or a means, cannot be made successfully among our intimate friends. These wretches know all about us—have seen through us long ago. With them we are, accordingly, quite natural. That is why we find their company so restful. Among acquaintances the pretence is worth making. But those who know anything at all about us are apt to find us out. That is why we find acquaintances such a nuisance. Among perfect strangers, who know nothing at all about us, we start with a clean slate. If our pretence do not come off, we have only ourselves to blame. And so we 'bluff' these strangers, blithely, for all we are worth, whether there be anything to gain or nothing. We all do it. Let us despise ourselves for doing it, but not one another. By which I mean, reader, do not be hard on me for making a show of my labels in railway-carriages. After all, the question is whether a man 'bluff' well or ill. If he brag vulgarly before his strangers, away with him! by all means. He does not know how to play the game. He is a failure. But, if he convey subtly (and, therefore, successfully) the fine impression he wishes to convey, then you should stifle your wrath, and try to pick up a few hints. When I saw my fellow-passengers eyeing my hat-box, I did not, of course, say aloud to them, 'Yes, mine is a delightful life! Any amount of money, any amount of leisure! And, what's more, I know how to make the best use of them both!' Had I done so, they would have immediately seen through me as an impostor. But I did nothing of the sort. I let my labels proclaim distinction for me, quietly, in their own way. And they made their proclamation with immense success. But there came among them, in course of time, one label that would not harmonise with them. Came, at length, one label that did me actual discredit. I happened to have had influenza, and my doctor had ordered me to make my convalescence in a place which, according to him, was better than any other for my particular condition. He had ordered me to Ramsgate, and to Ramsgate I had gone. A label on my hat-box duly testified to my obedience. At the time, I had thought nothing of it. But, in subsequent journeys, I noticed that my hat-box did not make its old effect, somehow. My fellow-passengers looked at it, were interested in it; but I had a subtle sense that they were not reverencing me as of yore. Something was the matter. I was not long in tracing what it was. The discord struck by Ramsgate was the more disastrous because, in my heedlessness, I had placed that ignoble label within an inch of my point d'appui—the trinity of Oxford, Newmarket and Assisi. What was I to do? I could not explain to my fellow-passengers, as I have explained to you, my reason for Ramsgate. So long as the label was there, I had to rest under the hideous suspicion of having gone there for pleasure, gone of my own free will. I did rest under it during the next two or three journeys. But the injustice of my position maddened me. At length, a too obvious sneer on the face of a fellow-passenger steeled me to a resolve that I would, for once, break my rule against obliteration. On the return journey, I obliterated Ramsgate with the new label, leaving visible merely the final TE, which could hardly compromise me.

Steterunt those two letters because I was loth to destroy what was, primarily, a symbol for myself: I wished to remember Ramsgate, even though I had to keep it secret. Only in a secondary, accidental way was my collection meant for the public eye. Else, I should not have hesitated to deck the hat-box with procured symbols of Seville, Simla, St. Petersburg and other places which I had not (and would have liked to be supposed to have) visited. But my collection was, first of all, a private autobiography, a record of my scores of Fate; and thus positively to falsify it would have been for me as impossible as cheating at 'Patience.' From that to which I would not add I hated to subtract anything—even Ramsgate. After all, Ramsgate was not London; to have been in it was a kind of score. Besides, it had restored me to health. I had no right to rase it utterly.

But such tendresse was not my sole reason for sparing those two letters. Already I was reaching that stage where the collector loves his specimens not for their single sakes, but as units in the sum-total. To every collector comes, at last, a time when he does but value his collection—how shall I say?—collectively. He who goes in for beautiful things begins, at last, to value his every acquisition not for its beauty, but because it enhances the worth of the rest. Likewise, he who goes in for autobiographic symbols begins, at last, to care not for the symbolism of another event in his life, but for the addition to the objects already there. He begins to value every event less for its own sake than because it swells his collection. Thus there came for me a time when I looked forward to a journey less because it meant movement and change for myself than because it meant another label for my hat-box. A strange state to fall into? Yes, collecting is a mania, a form of madness. And it is the most pleasant form of madness in the whole world. It can bring us nearer to real happiness than can any form of sanity. The normal, eclectic man is never happy, because he is always craving something of another kind than what he has got. The collector, in his mad concentration, wants only more and more of what he has got already; and what he has got already he cherishes with a passionate joy. I cherished my gallimaufry of rainbow-coloured labels almost as passionately as the miser his hoard of gold. Why do we call the collector of current coin a miser? Wretched? He? True, he denies himself all the reputed pleasures of life; but does he not do so of his own accord, gladly? He sacrifices everything to his mania; but that merely proves how intense his mania is. In that the nature of his collection cuts him off from all else, he is the perfect type of the collector. He is above all other collectors. And he is the truly happiest of them all. It is only when, by some merciless stroke of Fate, he is robbed of his hoard, that he becomes wretched. Then, certainly, he suffers. He suffers proportionately to his joy. He is smitten with sorrow more awful than any sorrow to be conceived by the sane. I whose rainbow-coloured hoard has been swept from me, seem to taste the full savour of his anguish.

I sit here thinking of the misers who, in life or in fiction, have been despoiled. Three only do I remember: Melanippus of Sicyon, Pierre Baudouin of Limoux, Silas Marner. Melanippus died of a broken heart. Pierre Baudouin hanged himself. The case of Silas Marner is more cheerful. He, coming into his cottage one night, saw by the dim light of the hearth, that which seemed to be his gold restored, but was really nothing but the golden curls of a little child, whom he was destined to rear under his own roof, finding in her more than solace for his bereavement. But then, he was a character in fiction: the other two really existed. What happened to him will not happen to me. Even if little children with rainbow-coloured hair were so common that one of them might possibly be left on my hearth-rug, I know well that I should not feel recompensed by it, even if it grew up to be as fascinating a paragon as Eppie herself. Had Silas Marner really existed (nay! even had George Eliot created him in her maturity) neither would he have felt recompensed. Far likelier, he would have been turned to stone, in the first instance, as was poor Niobe when the divine arrows destroyed that unique collection on which she had lavished so many years. Or, may be, had he been a very strong man, he would have found a bitter joy in saving up for a new hoard. Like Carlyle, when the MS. of his masterpiece was burned by the housemaid of John Stuart Mill, he might have begun all over again, and built a still nobler monument on the tragic ashes.

That is a fine, heartening example! I will be strong enough to follow it. I will forget all else. I will begin all over again. There stands my hat-box! Its glory is departed, but I vow that a greater glory awaits it. Bleak, bare and prosaic it is now, but—ten years hence! Its career, like that of the Imperial statesman in the moment of his downfall, 'is only just beginning.'

There is a true Anglo-Saxon ring in this conclusion. May it appease whomever my tears have been making angry.

GENERAL ELECTIONS

I admire detachment. I commend a serene indifference to hubbub. I like Archimedes, Leonardo da Vinci, Goethe, Balzac, Darwin, and other sages, for having been so concentrated on this or that eternal verity in art or science or philosophy, that they paid no heed to alarums and excursions which were sweeping all other folk off their feet. It is with some shame that I haunt the tape-machine whenever a General Election is going on.

Of politics I know nothing. My mind is quite open on the subject of fiscal reform, and quite empty; and the void is not an aching one: I have no desire to fill it. The idea of the British Empire leaves me quite cold. If this or that subject race threw off our yoke, I should feel less vexation than if one comma were misplaced in the printing of this essay. The only feeling that our Colonies inspire in me is a determination not to visit them. Socialism neither affrights nor attracts me—or, rather, it has both these effects equally. When I think of poverty and misery crushing the greater part of humanity, and most of all when I hear of some specific case of distress, I become a socialist indeed. But I am not less an artist than a human being, and when I think of Demos, that chin-bearded god, flushed with victory, crowned with leaflets of the Social Democratic League, quaffing temperance beverages in a world all drab; when I think of model lodging-houses in St. James's Park, and trams running round and round St. James's Square—the mighty fallen, and the lowly swollen, and, in Elysium, the shade of Matthew Arnold shedding tears on the shoulder of a shade so different as George Brummell's—tears, idle tears, at sight of the Barbarians, whom he had mocked and loved, now annihilated by those others whom he had mocked and hated; when such previsions as these come surging up in me, I do deem myself well content with the present state of things, dishonourable though it is. As to socialism, then, you see, my mind is evenly divided. It is with no political bias that I go and hover around the tape-machine. My interest in General Elections is a merely 'sporting' interest. I do not mean that I lay bets. A bad fairy decreed over my cradle that I should lose every bet that I might make; and, in course of time, I abandoned a practice which took away from coming events the pleasing element of uncertainty. 'A merely dramatic interest' is less equivocal, and more accurate.

'This,' you say, 'is rank incivism.' I assume readily that you are an ardent believer in one political party or another, and that, having studied thoroughly all the questions at issue, you could give cogent reasons for all the burning faith that is in you. But how about your friends and acquaintances? How many of them can cope with you in discussion? How many of them show even a desire to cope with you? Travel, I beg you, on the Underground Railway, or in a Tube. Such places are supposed to engender in their passengers a taste for political controversy. Yet how very elementary are such arguments as you will hear there! It is obvious that these gentlemen know and care very little about 'burning questions.' What they do know and care about is the purely personal side of politics. They have their likes and their dislikes for a few picturesque and outstanding figures. These they will attack or defend with fervour. But you will be lucky if you overhear any serious discussion of policy. Emerge from the nether world. Range over the whole community—from the costermonger who says 'Good Old Winston!' to the fashionable woman who says 'I do think Mr. Balfour is rather wonderful!'—and you will find the same plentiful lack of interest in the impersonal side of politics. You will find that almost every one is interested in politics only as a personal conflict between certain interesting men—as a drama, in fact. Frown not, then, on me alone.

Whenever a General Election occurs, the conflict becomes sharper and more obvious—the play more exciting—the audience more tense. The stage is crowded with supernumeraries, not interesting in themselves, but adding a new interest to the merely personal interest. There is the stronger 'side,' here the weaker, ranged against each other. Which will be vanquished? It rests with the audience to decide. And, as human nature is human nature, of course the audience decides that the weaker side shall be victorious. That is what politicians call 'the swing of the pendulum.' They believe that the country is alienated by the blunders of the Government, and is disappointed by the unfulfilment of promises, and is anxious for other methods of policy. Bless them! the country hardly noticed their blunders, has quite forgotten their promises, and cannot distinguish between one set of methods and another. When the man in the street sees two other men in the street fighting, he doesn't care to know the cause of the combat: he simply wants the smaller man to punish the bigger, and to punish him with all possible severity. When a party with a large majority appeals to the country, its appeal falls, necessarily, on deaf ears. Some years ago there happened an exception to this rule. But then the circumstances were exceptional. A small nation was fighting a big nation, and, as the big nation happened to be yourselves, your sympathy was transferred to the big nation. As the little party was suspected of favouring the little nation, your sympathy was transferred likewise to the big party. Barring 'khaki,' sympathy takes its usual course in General Elections. The bigger the initial majority, the bigger the collapse. It is not enough that Goliath shall fall: he must bite the dust, and bite plenty of it. It is not enough that David shall have done what he set out to do: a throne must be found for this young man. Away with the giant's body! Hail, King David!

I should like to think that chivalry was the sole motive of our zeal. I am afraid that the mere craving for excitement has something to do with it. Pelion has never been piled on Ossa; and no really useful purpose could be served by the superimposition. But we should like to see the thing done. It would appeal to our sense of the grandiose—our hankering after the unlimited. When the man of science shows us a drop of water in a test-tube, and tells us that this tiny drop contains more than fifteen billions of infusoria, we are subtly gratified, and cherish a secret hope that the number of infusoria is very much more than fifteen billions. In the same way, we hope that the number of seats gained by the winning party will be even greater to-morrow than it is to-day. 'We are sweeping the country,' exclaims (say) the professed Liberal; and at the word 'sweeping' there is in his eyes a gleam that no mere party feeling could have lit there. It is a gleam that comes from the very depths of his soul—a reflection of the innate human passion for breaking records, or seeing them broken, no matter how or why. 'Yes,' says the professed Tory, 'you certainly are sweeping the country.' He tries to put a note of despondency into his voice; but hark how he rolls the word 'sweeping' over his tongue! He, too, though he may not admit it, is longing to creep into the smoking-room of the National Liberal Club and feast his eyes on the blazing galaxy of red seals affixed to the announcements of the polling. He turns to his evening paper, and reads again the list of ex-Cabinet ministers who have been unseated. He feels, in his heart of hearts, what fun it would be if they had all been unseated. He grudges the exceptions. For political bias is one thing; human nature another.

A PARALLEL

The club-room looked very like the auditorium of a music-hall. Indeed, that is what it must once have been. But now there were tiers of benches on the stage; and on these was packed a quarter or so of the members and their friends. The other three-quarters or so were packed opposite the proscenium and down either side of the hall. And in the middle of this human oblong was a raised platform, roped around. Therefrom, just as I was ushered to my place, a stout man in evening dress was making some announcement. I did not catch its import; but it was loudly applauded. The stout man—most of the audience indeed, seemed to have put on flesh—bowed himself off, and disappeared from my ken in the clouds of tobacco-smoke that hung about the hall. Almost immediately, two young people, nimbly insinuating themselves through the rope fence, leapt upon the platform. One was a man of about twenty years of age; the other, a girl of about seventeen. She was very pretty; he was very handsome; both were becomingly dressed, with evident aim at attractiveness. They proceeded to opposite corners of the platform. At a signal from some one, they advanced to the middle; and each made a hideous grimace at the other. The grimace, strange in itself, was stranger still in the light of what followed. For the young man began to make passionate protestations of love, to which the girl responded with equal ardour. The young man fell to his knees; the girl raised him, and clung to his breast. His language became more and more lyrical, his eyes more and more ecstatic. Suddenly in the middle of a pretty sentence, wherein his love was likened to a flight of doves, a bell rang; whereat, not less abruptly, the couple separated, retiring to the aforesaid corners of the platform and sinking back on their chairs with every manifestation of fatigue. Their friends or attendants, however, rallied round them, counselling them, cooling them with fans, heartening them to fresh endeavour; and when, at the end of a minute, the signal was sounded for a second tryst, the two young people seemed fresher and more eager than ever. This time, most of the love-making was done by the girl; the young man joyously drinking in her words, and now and then interpolating a few of his own. There were four trysts in all, with three intervals for recuperation. At the fourth sound of the bell, the lovers, stepping asunder, repeated their hideous mutual grimace, and disappeared from the platform as suddenly as they had come. Their place was soon taken by another, a more mature, and heavier, but not less personable, couple, who proceeded to make love in their own somewhat different way. The lyrical notes seemed to be missing in them. But maturity, though it had stripped away magic, had not blunted their passion—had, rather, sharpened the edge of it, and made it a stronger and more formidable instrument. Throughout the evening, indeed, in the long succession that there was of amorous encounters, it seemed to be the encounters of mature couples that excited in the smoke-laden audience the keenest interest. It was evidently not etiquette to interrupt the lovers while they were talking; but, whenever the bell sounded, there was a frantic outburst of sympathy, straight from the heart; and sometimes, even while a love-scene was proceeding, this or that stout gentleman would snatch the cigar from his lips and emit a heart-cry. Now and again, it seemed to be thought that the lovers were insufficiently fervid—were but dallying with passion; and then there were stentorian grunts of disapproval and hortation. I did not gather that the audience itself was composed mainly of active lovers. I guessed that the greater number consisted of men who do but take an active interest in other people's love affairs—men who, vigilant from a detached position, have developed in themselves an extraordinarily sound critical knowledge of what is due to Venus. 'Plaisir d'amour ne dure qu'un moment,' I murmured; 'chagrin d'amour dure toute la vie. And wise are ye who, immune from all love's sorrow, win incessant joy in surveying Cythara through telescopes. Suave mari magno,' I murmured. And this second tag caused me to awake from my dream shivering.

A strange dream? Yet a precisely parallel reality had inspired it. I had been taken over-night—my first visit—to the National Sporting Club.

The instinct to fight, like the instinct to love, is a quite natural instinct. To fight and to love are the primary instincts of primitive man. I know that people with strongly amorous natures are not trained and paid to make love ceremoniously, in accordance to certain rules laid down for them by certain authorities, and for the delectation of highly critical audiences. But, if this custom prevailed, it would not seem to me stranger than the custom of training and paying pugnacious people to hit one another on the face and breast, with the greatest possible skill and violence, for the delectation of highly critical audiences. I do not say that a glove-fight is in itself a visually disgusting exhibition. I saw no blood spilt, the other night, and no bruises expressed, by either the 'light-weights' or the 'heavy-weights.' I dare say, too, that the fighters enjoy their profession, on the whole. But I contend that it is a very lamentable profession, in that it depends on the calculated prostitution of good natural energies. A declaration of love prefaced by a grimace, such as I saw in my dream, seems to me not one whit more monstrous than a violent onslaught prefaced by a hand-shake. If two men are angry with each other, let them fight it out (provided I be not one of them) in the good old English fashion, by all means. But prize-fighting is to be deplored as an offence against the soul of man. And this offence is committed, not by the fighters themselves, but by us soft and sedentary gentlemen who set them on to fight. Looking back at ancient Rome, no one blames the poor gladiators in the arena. Every one reserves his pious horror for the citizens in the amphitheatre. Yet how are we superior to them? Are we not even as they—

suspended at exactly their point between barbarism and civilisation. In course of time, doubtless, 'the ring' will die out. For either we shall become so civilised that we shall not rejoice in the sight of painful violence, or we shall relapse into barbarism and go into the mauling business on our own account. Our present stage—the stage of our transition—is not pretty, I think.

A MORRIS FOR MAY-DAY

Not long ago a prospectus was issued by some more or less aesthetic ladies and gentlemen who, deeming modern life not so cheerful as it should be, had laid their cheerless heads together and decided that they would meet once every month and dance old-fashioned dances in a hall hired for the purpose. Thus would they achieve a renascence—I am sure they called it a renascence—of 'Merrie England.' I know not whether subscriptions came pouring in. I know not even whether the society ever met. If it ever did meet, I conceive that its meetings must have been singularly dismal. If you are depressed by modern life, you are unlikely to find an anodyne in the self-appointed task of cutting certain capers which your ancestors used to cut because they, in their day, were happy. If you think modern life so pleasant a thing that you involuntarily prance, rather than walk, down the street, I dare say your prancing will intensify your joy. Though I happen never to have met him out-of-doors, I am sure my friend Mr. Gilbert Chesterton always prances thus—prances in some wild way symbolical of joy in modern life. His steps, and the movements of his arms and body, may seem to you crude, casual, and disconnected at first sight; but that is merely because they are spontaneous. If you studied them carefully, you would begin to discern a certain rhythm, a certain harmony. You would at length be able to compose from them a specific dance—a dance not quite like any other—a dance formally expressive of new English optimism. If you are not optimistic, don't hope to become so by practising the steps. But practise them assiduously if you are; and get your fellow-optimists to practise them with you. You will grow all the happier through ceremonious expression of a light heart. And your children and your children's children will dance 'The Chesterton' when you are no more. May be, a few of them will still be dancing it now and then, on this or that devious green, even when optimism shall have withered for ever from the land. Nor will any man mock at the survival. The dance will have lost nothing of its old grace, and will have gathered that quality of pathos which makes even unlovely relics dear to us—that piteousness which Time gives ever to things robbed of their meaning and their use. Spectators will love it for its melancholy not less than for its beauty. And I hope no mere spectator will be so foolish as to say, 'Let us do it' with a view to reviving cheerfulness at large. I hope it will be held sacred to those in whom it will be a tradition—a familiar thing handed down from father to son. None but they will be worthy of it. Others would ruin it. Be sure I trod no measure with the Morris-dancers whom I saw last May-day.

It was in the wide street of a tiny village near Oxford that I saw them. Fantastic—high-fantastical—figures they did cut in their finery. But in demeanour they were quite simple, quite serious, these eight English peasants. They had trudged hither from the neighbouring village that was their home. And they danced quite simply, quite seriously. One of them, I learned, was a cobbler, another a baker, and the rest were farm-labourers. And their fathers and their fathers' fathers had danced here before them, even so, every May-day morning. They were as deeply rooted in antiquity as the elm outside the inn. They were here always in their season as surely as the elm put forth its buds. And the elm, knowing them, approving them, let its green-flecked branches dance in unison with them.

The first dance was in full swing when I approached. Only six of the men were dancers. Of the others, one was the 'minstrel,' the other the 'dysard.' The minstrel was playing a flute; and the dysard I knew by the wand and leathern bladder which he brandished as he walked around, keeping a space for the dancers, and chasing and buffeting merrily any man or child who ventured too near. He, like the others, wore a white smock decked with sundry ribands, and a top-hat that must have belonged to his grandfather. Its antiquity of form and texture contrasted strangely with the freshness of the garland of paper roses that wreathed it. I was told that the wife or sweetheart of every Morris-dancer takes special pains to deck her man out more gaily than his fellows. But this pious endeavour had defeated its own end. So bewildering was the amount of brand-new bunting attached to all these eight men that no matron or maiden could for the life of her have determined which was the most splendid of them all. Besides his adventitious finery, every dancer, of course, had in his hands the scarves which are as necessary to his performance of the Morris as are the bells strapped about the calves of his legs. Waving these scarves and jangling these bells with a stolid rhythm, the six peasants danced facing one another, three on either side, while the minstrel fluted and the dysard strutted around. That minstrel's tune runs in my head even now—a queer little stolid tune that recalls vividly to me the aspect of the dance. It is the sort of tune Bottom the Weaver must often have danced to in his youth. I wish I could hum it for you on paper. I wish I could set down for you on paper the sight that it conjures up. But what writer that ever lived has been able to write adequately about a dance? Even a slow, simple dance, such as these peasants were performing, is a thing that not the cunningest writer could fix in words. Did not Flaubert say that if he could describe a valse he would die happy? I am sure he would have said this if it had occurred to him.

Unable to make you see the Morris, how can I make you feel as I felt in seeing it? I cannot explain even to myself the effect it had on me. My critics have often complained of me that I lack 'heart'—presumably the sort of heart that is pronounced with a rolling of the r; and I suppose they are right. I remember having read the death of Little Nell on more than one occasion without floods of tears. How can I explain to myself the tears that came into my eyes at sight of the Morris? They are not within the rubric of the tears drawn by mere contemplation of visual beauty. The Morris, as I saw it, was curious, antique, racy, what you will: not beautiful. Nor was there any obvious pathos in it. Often, in London, passing through some slum where a tune was being ground from an organ, I have paused to watch the little girls dancing. In the swaying dances of these wan, dishevelled, dim little girls I have discerned authentic beauty, and have wondered where they had learned the grace of their movements, and where the certainty with which they did such strange and complicated steps. Surely, I have thought, this is no trick of to-day or yesterday: here, surely, is the remainder of some old tradition; here, may be, is Merrie England, run to seed. There is an obvious pathos in the dances of these children of the gutter—an obvious symbolism of sadness, of a wistful longing for freedom and fearlessness, for wind and sunshine. No wonder that at sight of it even so heartless a person as the present writer is a little touched. But why at sight of those rubicund, full-grown, eupeptic Morris-dancers on the vernal highroad? No obvious pathos was diffusing itself from them. They were Merrie England in full flower. In part, I suppose, my tears were tears of joy for the very joyousness of these men; in part, of envy for their fine simplicity; in part, of sorrow in the thought that they were a survival of the past, not types of the present, and that their knell would soon be tolled, and the old elm see their like no more.

After they had drunk some ale, they formed up for the second dance—a circular dance. And anon, above the notes of the flute and the jangling of the bells and the stamping of the boots, I seemed to hear the knell actually tolling, Hoot! Hoot! Hoot! A motor came fussing and fuming in its cloud of dust. Hoot! Hoot! The dysard ran to meet it, brandishing his wand of office. He had to stand aside. Hoot! The dancers had just time to get out of the way. The scowling motorists vanished. Dancers and dysard, presently visible through the subsiding dust, looked rather foolish and crestfallen. And all the branches of the conservative old elm above them seemed to be quivering with indignation.

In a sense this elm was a mere parvenu as compared with its beloved dancers. True, it had been no mere sapling in the reign of the seventh Henry, and so could remember distinctly the first Morris danced here. But the first Morris danced on English soil was not, by a long chalk, the first Morris. Scarves such as these were waved, and bells such as these were jangled, and some such measure as this was trodden, in the mists of a very remote antiquity. Spanish buccaneers, long before the dawn of the fifteenth century, had seen the Moors dancing somewhat thus to the glory of Allah. Home-coming, they had imitated that strange and savage dance, expressive, for them, of the joy of being on firm native land again. The 'Morisco' they called it; and it was much admired; and the fashion of it spread throughout Spain—scaled the very

Pyrenees, and invaded France. To the 'Maurisce' succumbed 'tout Paris' as quickly as in recent years it succumbed to the cake-walk. A troupe of French dancers braved the terrors of the sea, and, with their scarves and their bells, danced for the delectation of the English court. 'The Kynge,' it seems, 'was pleased by the bels and sweet dauncing.' Certain of his courtiers 'did presentlie daunce so in open playces.' No one with any knowledge of the English nature will be surprised to hear that the cits soon copied the courtiers. But 'the Morrice was not for longe practysed in the cittie. It went to countrie playces.' London, apparently, even in those days, did not breed joy in life. The Morris sought and found its proper home in the fields and by the wayside. Happy carles danced it to the glory of God, even as it had erst been danced to the glory of Allah.

It was no longer, of course, an explicitly religious dance. But neither can its origin have been explicitly religious. Every dance, however formal it become later, begins as a mere ebullition of high spirits. The Dionysiac dances began in the same way as 'the Chesterton.' Some Thessalian vintner, say, suddenly danced for sheer joy that the earth was so bounteous; and his fellow vintners, sharing his joy, danced with him; and ere their breath was spent they remembered who it was that had given them such cause for merry-making, and they caught leaves from the vine and twined them in their hair, and from the fig-tree and the fir-tree they snatched branches, and waved them this way and that, as they danced, in honour of him who was lord of these trees and of this wondrous vine. Thereafter this dance of joy became a custom, ever to be observed at certain periods of the year. It took on, beneath its joyousness, a formal solemnity. It was danced slowly around an altar of stone, whereon wood and salt were burning—burning with little flames that were pale in the sunlight. Formal hymns were chanted around this altar. And some youth, clad in leopard's skin and wreathed with ivy, masqueraded as the god himself, and spoke words appropriate to that august character. It was from these beginnings that sprang the art-form of drama. The Greeks never hid the origin of this their plaything. Always in the centre of the theatre was the altar to Dionysus; and the chorus, circling around it, were true progeny of those old agrestic singers; and the mimes had never been but for that masquerading youth. It is hard to realise, yet it is true, that we owe to the worship of Dionysus so dreary a thing as the modern British drama. Strange that through him who gave us the juice of the grape, 'fiery, venerable, divine,' came this gift too! Yet I dare say the chorus of a musical comedy would not be awestruck—would, indeed, 'bridle'—if one unrolled to them their illustrious pedigree.

The history of the Dionysiac dance has a fairly exact parallel in that of the 'Morisco.' Each dance has travelled far, and survives, shorn of its explicitly religious character, and in many other ways 'diablement change' en route.'

The 'Morisco,' of course, has changed the less of the two. Besides the scarves and the bells, it seemed to me last May-day that the very steps danced and figures formed were very like to those of which I had read, and which I had seen illustrated in old English and French engravings. Above all, the dancers seemed to retain, despite their seriousness, something of the joy in which the dance originated. They frowned as they footed it, but they were evidently happy. Their frowns did but betoken determination to do well and rightly a thing that they loved doing—were proud of doing. The smiles of the chorus in a musical comedy seem but to express depreciation of a rather tedious and ridiculous exercise. The coryphe'es are quite evidently bored and ashamed. But these eight be-ribanded sons of the soil were hardly less glad in dancing than was that antique Moor who, having slain beneath the stars some long-feared and long-hated enemy, danced wildly on the desert sand, and, to make music, tore strips of bells from his horse's saddle and waved them in either hand while he danced, and made so great a noise in the night air that other Moors came riding to see what had happened, and marvelled at the sight and sound of the dance, and, praising Allah, leapt down and tore strips of bells from their own saddles, and danced as nearly as they could in mimicry of that glad conqueror, to Allah's glory.

As this scene is mobled in the aforesaid mists of antiquity, I cannot vouch for the details. Nor can I say just when the Moors found that they could make a finer and more rhythmic jangle by attaching the bells to their legs than by swinging them in their hands. Nor can I fix the day when they tore strips from their turbans for their idle hands to wave. I cannot say how long the rite's mode had been set when first the adventurers from Spain beheld it with their keen wondering eyes and fixed it for ever in their memories.

In Spain, and then in France, and then in London, the dance was secular. But perhaps I ought not to have said that it was 'not explicitly religious' in the English countryside. The cult for Robin Hood was veritably a religion throughout the Midland Counties. Rites in his honour were performed on certain days of the year with a not less hearty reverence, a not less quaint elaboration, than was infused into the rustic Greek rites for Dionysus. The English carles danced, not indeed around an altar, but around a bunt pole crowned with such flowers as were in season; and one of them, like the youth who in the Dionysiac dance masqueraded as the god, was decked out duly as Robin Hood—'with a magpye's plume to hys capp,' we are told, and sometimes 'a russat bearde compos'd of horses hair.' The most famous of the dances for Robin Hood was the 'pageant.' Herein appeared, besides the hero himself and various tabours and pipers, a 'dysard' or fool, and Friar Tuck, and Maid Marian—'in a white kyrtele and her hair all unbrayded, but with blossoms thereyn.' This 'pageant' was performed at Whitsun, at Easter, on New-Year's day, and on May-day. The Morris, when it had become known in the villages, was very soon incorporated in the 'pageant.' The Morris scarves and bells, the Morris steps and figures, were all pressed into the worship of Robin Hood. In most villages the properties for the 'pageant' had always rested in the custody of the church-wardens. The properties for the Morris were now kept with them. In the Kingston accounts for 1537-8 are enumerated 'a fryers cote of russat, and a kyrtele weltyd with red cloth, a Mowrens cote of buckram, and four morres daunsars cotes of white fustian spangelid, and two gryne saten cotes, and disarddes cote of cotton, and six payre of garters with belles.' The 'pageant' itself fell, little by little, into disuse; the Morris, which had been affiliated to it, superseded it. Of the 'pageant' nothing remained but the minstrel and the dysard and an occasional Maid Marian. In the original Morris there had been no music save that of the bells. But now there was always a flute or tabor. The dysard, with his rod and leathern bladder, was promoted to a sort of leadership. He did not dance, but gave the signal for the dance, and distributed praise or blame among the performers, and had power to degrade from the troupe any man who did not dance with enough skill or enough heartiness. Often there were in one village two rival troupes of dancers, and a prize was awarded to whichever acquitted itself the more admirably. But not only the 'ensemble' was considered. A sort of 'star system' seems to have crept in. Often a prize would be awarded to some one dancer who had excelled his fellows. There were, I suppose, 'born' Morris-dancers. Now and again, one of them, flushed with triumph, would secern himself from his troupe, and would 'star' round the country for his livelihood.

Such a one was Mr. William Kemp, who, at the age of seventeen, and in the reign of Queen Elizabeth, danced from his native village to London, where he educated himself and became an actor. Perhaps he was not a good actor, for he presently reverted to the Morris. He danced all the way from London to Norwich, and wrote a pamphlet about it—'Kemp's Nine Dajes' Wonder, performed in a daunce from London to Norwich. Containing the pleasures, paines, and kind entertainment of William Kemp betweene London and that Citty, in his late Morrice.' He seems to have encountered more pleasures than 'paines.' Gentle and simple, all the way, were very cordial. The gentle entertained him in their mansions by night. The simple danced with him by day. In Sudbury 'there came a lusty tall fellow, a butcher by his profession, that would in a Morice keepe me company to Bury. I gave him thankes, and forward wee did set; but ere ever wee had measur'd halfe a mile of our way, he gave me over in the plain field, protesting he would not hold out with me; for, indeed, my pace in dauncing is not ordinary. As he and I were parting, a lusty country lasse being among the people, cal'd him faint-hearted lout, saying, "If I had begun to daunce, I would have held out one myle, though it had cost my life." At which words many laughed. "Nay," saith she, "if the dauncer will lend me a leash of his belles, I'le venter to treade one myle with him myself." I lookt upon her, saw mirth in her eies, heard boldness in her words, and beheld her ready to tucke up her russat petticoate; and I fitted her with bels, which she merrily taking garnisht her thicke short legs, and with a smooth brow bad the tabur begin. The drum strucke; forward marcht I with my merry Mayde Marian, who shook her stout sides, and footed it merrily to Melford, being a long myle. There parting with her (besides her skinfull of drinke), and English crowne to buy more drinke; for, good wench, she was in a pittious heate; my kindness she requited with dropping a dozen good courtsies, and bidding God blesse the dauncer. I bade her adieu; and, to give her her due, she had a good eare, daunst truly, and wee parted friends.' Kemp, you perceive, wrote as well as he danced. I wish he had danced less and written more. It seems that he never wrote anything but this one delightful pamphlet. He died three years later, in the thirtieth year of his age—died dancing, with his bells on his legs, in the village of Ockley.

John Thorndrake, another professional Morris-dancer, was not so brilliant a personage as poor Kemp; but was of tougher fibre, it would seem. He died in his native town, Canterbury, at the age of seventy-eight; and had danced— never less than a mile, seldom less than five miles—every day, except Sunday, for sixty years. But even his record pales beside the account of a Morris that was danced by eight men, in Hereford, one May-day in the reign of James I. The united ages of these dancers, according to a contemporary pamphleteer, exceeded eight hundred years. The youngest of them was seventy-nine, and the ages of the rest ranged between ninety-five and a hundred and nine. 'And they daunced right well.' Of the hold that the Morris had on England, could there be stronger proof than in the feat of these indomitable dotards? The Morris ceased not even during the Civil Wars. Some of King Charles's men (according to Groby, the Puritan) danced thus on the eve of Naseby. Not even the Protectorate could stamp the Morris out, though we are told that Groby and other preachers throughout the land inveighed against it as 'lewde' and 'ungodlie.' The Restoration was in many places celebrated by special Morrises. The perihelion of this dance seems, indeed, to have been in the reign of Charles II. Georgian writers treated it somewhat as a survival, and were not always even tender to it. Says a writer in Bladud's Courier, describing a 'soire'e de beaute" given by Lady Jersey, 'Mrs. —— (la belle) looked as silly and gaudy, I do vow, as one of the old Morris Dancers.' And many other writers—from Horace Walpole to Captain Harver—have their sneer at the Morris. Its rusticity did not appeal to the polite Georgian mind; and its Moorishness, which would have appealed strongly, was overlooked. Still, the Morris managed to survive urban disdain—was still dear to the carles whose fathers had taught it them.

And long may it linger!

THE HOUSE OF COMMONS MANNER

A grave and beautiful place, the Palace of Westminster. I sometimes go to that little chamber of it wherein the Commons sit sprawling or stand spouting. I am a constant reader of the 'graphic reports' of what goes on in the House of Commons; and the writers of these things always strive to give one the impression that nowhere is the human comedy so fast and furious, nowhere played with such skill and brio, as at St. Stephen's; and I am rather easily influenced by anything that appears in daily print, for I have a burning faith in the sagacity and uprightness of sub-editors; and so, when the memory of my last visit to the House has lost its edge, and when there is a crucial debate in prospect, to the House I go, full of hope that this time I really shall be edified or entertained. With an open mind I go, reeking naught of the pro's and con's of the subject of the debate. I go as to a gladiatorial show, eager to applaud any man who shall wield his sword brilliantly. If a 'stranger' indulge in applause, he is tapped on the shoulder by one of those courteous, magpie-like officials, and conducted beyond the precincts of the Palace of Westminster. I speak from hearsay. I do not think I have ever seen a 'stranger' applauding. My own hands, certainly, never have offended.

Years ago, when to be a member of the House of Commons was to be (or to deem oneself) a personage of great importance, the debates were conducted with a keen eye to effect. Members who had a sense of beauty made their speeches beautiful, and even those to whom it was denied did their best. Grace of ample gesture was cultivated, and sonorous elocution, and lucid ordering of ideas, and noble language. In fact, there was a school of oratory. This is no mere superstition, bred of man's innate tendency to exalt the past above the present. It is a fact that can easily be verified through contemporary records. It is a fact which I myself have verified in the House with my own eyes and ears. More than once, I heard there—and it was a pleasure and privilege to hear—a speech made by Sir William Harcourt. And from his speeches I was able to deduce the manner of his coevals and his forerunners. Long past his prime he was, and bearing up with very visible effort against his years. An almost extinct volcano! But sufficient to imagination these glimpses of the glow that had been, and the sight of these last poor rivulets of the old lava. An almost extinct volcano, but majestic among mole-hills! Assuredly, the old school was a fine one. It had its faults, of course—floridness, pomposity, too much histrionism. It was, indeed, very like the old school of acting, in its defects as in its qualities. With all his defects, what a relief it is to see one of the old actors among a cast of new ones! How he takes the stage, making himself felt—and heard! How surely he achieves his effects in the grand manner! Robustious? Yes. But it is better to exaggerate a style than to have no style at all. That is what is the matter with these others—these quiet, shifty, shamefaced others they have no style at all. And as is the difference between the old actor and them, so, precisely was the difference between Sir William Harcourt and the modern members.

I do not desire the new actors to model themselves on the old, whose manner is quite incongruous with the character of modern drama. All I would have them do is to achieve the manner for which they are darkly fumbling. Even so, I do not demand oratory of the modern senators. Oratory I love, but I admit that the time for it is bygone. It belonged to the age of port. On plenty of port the orator spoke, and on plenty of port his audience listened to him. A diet-bound generation can hardly produce an orator; and if, by some mysterious throw-back, an orator actually is produced, he falls very flat. There was in my college at Oxford a little 'Essay Society,' to which I found myself belonging. We used to meet every Thursday evening in the room of this or that member; and, when coffee had been handed round, one of us read an essay—a calm little mild essay on one of those vast themes that no undergraduate can resist. After this, we had a calm little mild discussion 'It seems to me that the reader of the paper has hardly laid enough stress on...' One of these evenings I can recall most distinctly. A certain freshman had been elected. The man who was to have read an essay had fallen ill, and the freshman had been asked to step into the breach. This he did, with an essay on 'The Ideals of Mazzini,' and with strange and terrific effect. During the exordium we raised our eyebrows. Presently we were staring open-mouthed. Where were we? In what wild dream were we drifting? To this day I can recite the peroration. Mazzini is dead. But his spirit lives, and can never be crushed. And his motto—the motto that he planted on the gallant banner of the Italian Republic, and sealed with his life's blood, remains, and shall remain, till, through the eternal ages, the universal air re-echoes to the inspired shout—'GOD AND THE PEOPLE!'

The freshman had begun to read his essay in a loud, declamatory style; but gradually, knowing with an orator's instinct, I suppose, that his audience was not 'with' him, he had quieted down, and become rather nervous—too nervous to skip, as I am sure he wished to skip, the especially conflagrant passages. But, as the end hove in sight, his confidence was renewed. A wave of emotion rose to sweep him ashore upon its crest. He gave the peroration for all it was worth. Mazzini is dead. I can hear now the hushed tone in which he spoke those words; the pause that followed them; and the gradual rising of his voice to a culmination at the words 'inspired shout'; and then another pause before that husky whisper 'GOD AND THE PEOPLE.' There was no discussion. We were petrified. We sat like stones; and presently, like shadows, we drifted out into the evening air. The little society met once or twice again; but any activity it still had was but the faint convulsion of a murdered thing. Old wine had been poured into a new bottle, with the usual result. Broken even so, belike, would be the glass roof of the Commons if a member spouted up to it such words as we heard that evening in Oxford. At any rate, the member would be howled down. So strong is the modern distaste for oratory. The day for oratory, as for toping, is past beyond redemption. 'Debating' is the best that can be done and appreciated by so abstemious a generation as ours. You will find a very decent level of 'debating' in the Oxford Union, in the Balham Ethical Society, in the Pimlico Parliament, and elsewhere. But not, I regret to say, in the House of Commons.

No one supposes that in a congeries of—how many?—six hundred and seventy men, chosen by the British public, there will be a very high average of mental capacity. If any one were so sanguine, a glance at the faces of our Conscript Fathers along the benches would soon bleed him. (I have no doubt that the custom of wearing hats in the House originated in the members' unwillingness to let strangers spy down on the shapes of their heads.) But it is not unreasonable to expect that the more active of these gentlemen will, through constant practice, not only in the senate, but also at elections and public dinners and so forth, have acquired a rough-and-ready professionalism in the art of speaking. It is not unreasonable to expect that they will be fairly fluent—fairly capable of arranging in logical sequence such ideas as they may have formed, and of reeling out words more or less expressive of these ideas. Well! certain of the Irishmen, certain of the Welshmen, proceed easily enough. But oh! those Saxon others! Look at them, hark at them, poor dears! See them clutching at their coats, and shuffling from foot to foot in travail, while their ideas—ridiculous mice, for the most part—get jerked painfully out somehow and anyhow. 'It seems to me that the Right—the honourable member for—er—er (the speaker dives to be prompted)—yes, of course—South Clapham—er—(temporising) the Southern division of Clapham—(long pause; his lips form the words 'Where was I?')—oh yes, the honourable gentleman the member for South Clapham seems to me to me—to be—in the position of one who, whilst the facts on which his propo—supposition are based—er—may or may not be in themselves acc—correct (gasps)—yet inasmuch—because—nevertheless...I should say rather—er—what it comes to is this: the honourable member for North—South Clapham seems to be labouring under a total, an entire, a complete (emphatic gesture, which throws him off his tack)—a contire—a complete disill—misunderstanding of the things which he himself relies on as—as—as a backing-up of the things that he would have us take or—er—accept and receive as the right sort of reduction—deduction from the facts of...in fact, from the facts of the case.' Then the poor dear heaves a deep sigh of relief, which is drowned by other members in a hideous cachinnation meant to express mirth.

And the odd thing is that the mirth is quite sincere and quite friendly. The speaker has just scored a point, though you mightn't think it. He has just scored a point in the true House of Commons manner. Possibly you have never been to the House of Commons, and suspect that I have caricatured its manner. Not at all. Indeed, to save space in these pages, I have rather improved it. If a phonograph were kept in the house, you would learn from it that the average sentence of the average speaker is an even more grotesque abortion than I have adumbrated. Happily for the prestige of the House, phonographs are excluded. Certain skilled writers—modestly dubbing themselves 'reporters'—are admitted, and by them cosmos is conjured out of chaos. 'The member for South Clapham appeared to be labouring under a misapprehension of the nature of the facts on which his argument was based (Laughter).' That is the finished article that your morning paper offers to you. And you, enjoying the delicious epigram over your tea and toast, are as unconscious of the toil that went to make it, and of the crises through which it passed, as you are of those poor sowers and reapers, planters and sailors and colliers, but for whom there would be no fragrant tea and toast for you.

The English are a naturally silent race. The most popular type of national hero is the 'strong silent man.' And most of the members of the House of Commons are, at any rate, silent members. Mercifully silent. Seeing the level attained by such members as have an impulse to speak, I shudder to conceive an oration by one of those unimpelled members... Perhaps I am too nervous. Surely I am too nervous. Surely the House of Commons manner cannot be a natural growth. Such perfect virtuosity in dufferdom can be acquired only by constant practice. But how comes it to be practised? I can only repeat that the English are a naturally silent race. They are apt to mistrust fluency. 'Glibness' they call it, and scent behind it the adventurer, the player of the confidence trick or the three-card trick, the robber of the widow and the orphan. Be smooth-tongued, and the Englishman will withdraw from you as quickly as may be, walking sideways like a crab, and looking askance at you with panic in his eyes. But stammer and blurt to him, and he will fall straight under the spell of your transparent honesty. A silly superstition; but there it is, ineradicable; and through it, undoubtedly, has come the house of Commons manner. Sometimes, through sheer nervousness, a new member achieves something like that manner; insomuch that his maiden speech is adjudged rich in promise, and 'the ear of the House' is assured to him when next he rises. Then is the dangerous time for him. He has conquered his nervousness now, but has not yet acquired that complex and delicate technique whereby a man can produce the illusion that he is striving hopelessly to utter something which, really, he could say with perfect ease. Thus he forfeits the sympathy of the House. Members stroll listlessly out. There is a buzz of conversation along the benches—perhaps the horrific refrain "Vide, 'Vide, 'Vide.' But the time will come when they shall hear him. Years hence—a beacon to show the heights that can be sealed by perseverance—he shall stand fumbling and floundering in a rapt senate.

Well! I take off my hat to virtuosity in any form. I admire Demosthenes, for whom pebbles in the mouth were a means to the end of oratory. I admire the Demosthenes de nos jours, for whom oratory is a means to the end of pebbles in the mouth. But I desire that the intelligent foreigner and the intelligent country cousin be not disappointed when they visit the House of Commons. Hitherto, strangers have expected to find there an exhibition of the art of speaking. That is the fault partly of those reporters to whom I have paid a well-deserved tribute. But it is more especially the fault of those other 'graphic' reporters, who write their lurid impressions of the debates. These gentlemen are most wildly misleading. I don't think they mislead you intentionally. If a man criticises one kind of ill-done thing exclusively, he cannot but, in course of time, lower his standard. Seeing nothing good, he will gradually forget what goodness is; and will accept as good that which is least bad. So it is with the graphic reporter in Parliament. He really does imagine that Hob 'raked the Treasury Bench with a merciless fire of raillery,' and that Nob 'went, as is his way, straight to the root of the subject,' and that Chittabob 'struck a deep note of pathos that will linger long in the memory of all who heard him.' If Hob, Nob, and Chittabob happen to be in opposition to the politics of the newspaper which he adorns, he will perhaps tell the truth about their respective performances. But he will tell it without believing it. All his geese are swans—bless him!—even when he won't admit it. The moral is that no man should be employed as graphic reporter for more than one session. Then the public would begin to learn the truth about St. Stephen's. Nor need the editors flinch from such a consummation. They used to entertain a theory that it was safest to have the productions at every theatre praised, in case any manager should withdraw his advertisements. But there need be no such fear in regard to St. Stephen's. That establishment does not advertise itself in the press as a place of amusement. Why should the press advertise it gratuitously?

For utility's sake, as well as for truth's, I would have the public enlightened. Exposed to ruthless criticism, our Commons might be shamed into an attempt at proficiency in the art of speaking. Then the sessions would be comparatively brief. After all, it is on the nation itself that falls the cost of lighting, warming, and ventilating St. Stephen's during the session. All the aforesaid dufferdom, therefore, increases the burden of the taxpayer. All those hum's and ha's mean so many pence from the pockets of you, reader, and me.

THE NAMING OF STREETS

'The Rebuilding of London' proceeds ruthlessly apace. The humble old houses that dare not scrape the sky are being duly punished for their timidity. Down they come; and in their place are shot up new tenements, quick and high as rockets. And the little old streets, so narrow and exclusive, so shy and crooked—we are making an example of them, too. We lose our way in them, do we?—we whose time is money. Our omnibuses can't trundle through them, can't they? Very well, then. Down with them! We have no use for them. This is the age of 'noble arteries.'

'The Rebuilding of London' is a source of much pride and pleasure to most of London's citizens, especially to them who are county councillors, builders, contractors, navvies, glaziers, decorators, and so forth. There is but a tiny residue of persons who do not swell and sparkle. And of these glum bystanders at the carnival I am one. Our aloofness is mainly irrational, I suppose. It is due mainly to temperamental Toryism. We say 'The old is better.' This we say to ourselves, every one of us feeling himself thereby justified in his attitude. But we are quite aware that such a postulate would not be accepted by time majority. For the majority, then, let us make some show of ratiocination. Let us argue that, forasmuch as London is an historic city, with many phases and periods behind her, and forasmuch as many of these phases and periods are enshrined in the aspect of her buildings, the constant rasure of these buildings is a disservice to the historian not less than to the mere sentimentalist, and that it will moreover (this is a more telling argument) filch from Englishmen the pleasant power of crowing over Americans, and from Americans the unpleasant necessity of balancing their pity for our present with envy of our past. After all, our past is our point d'appui. Our present is merely a bad imitation of what the Americans can do much better.

Ignoring as mere scurrility this criticism of London's present, but touched by my appeal to his pride in its history, the average citizen will reply, reasonably enough, to this effect: 'By all means let us have architectural evidence of our epochs—Caroline, Georgian, Victorian, what you will. But why should the Edvardian be ruled out? London is packed full of architecture already. Only by rasing much of its present architecture can we find room for commemorating duly the glorious epoch which we have just entered. To this reply there are two rejoinders: (1) let special suburbs be founded for Edvardian buildings; (2) there are no really Edvardian buildings, and there won't be any. Long before the close of the Victorian Era our architects had ceased to be creative. They could not express in their work the spirit of their time. They could but evolve a medley of old styles, some foreign, some native, all inappropriate. Take the case of Mayfair. Mayfair has for some years been in a state of transition. The old Mayfair, grim and sombre, with its air of selfish privacy and hauteur and leisure, its plain bricked facades, so disdainful of show—was it not redolent of the century in which it came to being? Its wide pavements and narrow roads between—could not one see in them the time when by day gentlemen and ladies went out afoot, needing no vehicle to whisk them to a destination, and walked to and fro amply, needing elbow-room for their dignity and their finery, and by night were borne in chairs, singly? And those queer little places of worship, those stucco chapels, with their very secular little columns, their ample pews, and their negligible altars over which one saw the Lion and the Unicorn fighting, as who should say, for the Cross—did they not breathe all the inimitable Erastianism of their period? In qua te qaero proseucha, my Lady Powderbox? Alas! every one of your tabernacles is dust now—dust turned to mud by the tears of the ghost of the Rev. Charles Honeyman, and by my own tears.... I have strayed again into sentiment. Back to the point—which is that the new houses and streets in Mayfair mean nothing. Let me show you Mount Street. Let me show you that airy stretch of sham antiquity, and defy you to say that it symbolises, how remotely soever, the spirit of its time. Mount Street is typical of the new Mayfair. And the new Mayfair is typical of the new London. In the height of these new houses, in the width of these new roads, future students will find, doubtless, something characteristic of this pressing and bustling age. But from the style of the houses he will learn nothing at all. The style might mean anything; and means, therefore, nothing. Original architecture is a lost art in England; and an art that is once lost is never found again. The Edvardian Era cannot be commemorated in its architecture.

Erection of new buildings robs us of the past and gives us in exchange nothing of the present. Consequently, the excuse put by me into the gaping mouth of the average Londoner cannot be accepted. I had no idea that my case was such a good one. Having now vindicated on grounds of patriotic utility that which I took to be a mere sentimental prejudice, I may be pardoned for dragging 'beauty' into the question. The new buildings are not only uninteresting through lack of temporal and local significance: they are also hideous. With all his learned eclecticism, the new architect seems unable to evolve a fake that shall be pleasing to the eye. Not at all pleasing is a mad hotch-potch of early Victorian hospital, Jacobean manor-house, Venetian palace, and bride-cake in Gunter's best manner. Yet that, apparently, is the modern English architect's pet ideal. Even when he confines himself to one manner, the result (even if it be in itself decent) is made horrible by vicinity to the work of a rival who has been dabbling in some other manner. Every street in London is being converted into a battlefield of styles, all shrieking at one another, all murdering one another. The tumult may be exciting, especially to the architects, but it is not beautiful. It is not good to live in.

However, I am no propagandist. I am not sanguine enough to suppose that I could do anything to stop either the adulteration or the demolition of old streets. I do not wish to infect the public with my own misgivings. On the contrary, my motive for this essay is to inoculate the public with my own placid indifference in a certain matter which seems always to cause them painful anxiety. Whenever a new highway is about to be opened, the newspapers are filled with letters suggesting that it ought to be called by this or that beautiful name, or by the name of this or that national hero. Well, in point of fact, a name cannot (in the long-run) make any shadow of difference in our sentiment for the street that bears it, for our sentiment is solely according to the character of the street itself; and, further, a street does nothing at all to keep green the memory of one whose name is given to it.

For a street one name is as good as another. To prove this proposition, let us proceed by analogy of the names borne by human beings. Surnames and Christian names may alike be divided into two classes: (1) those which, being identical with words in the dictionary, connote some definite thing; (2) those which, connoting nothing, may or may not suggest something by their sound. Instances of Christian names in the first class are Rose, Faith; of surnames, Lavender, Badger; of Christian names in the second class, Celia, Mary; of surnames, Jones, Vavasour. Let us consider the surnames in the first class. You will say, off-hand, that Lavender sounds pretty, and that Badger sounds ugly. Very well. Now, suppose that Christian names connoting unpleasant things were sometimes conferred at baptisms. Imagine two sisters named Nettle and Envy. Off-hand, you will say that these names sound ugly, whilst Rose and Faith sound pretty. Yet, believe me, there is not, in point of actual sound, one pin to choose either between Badger and Lavender, or between Rose and Nettle, or between Faith and Envy. There is no such thing as a singly euphonious or a singly cacophonous name. There is no word which, by itself, sounds ill or well. In combination, names or words may be made to sound ill or well. A sentence can be musical or unmusical. But in detachment words are no more preferable one to another in their sound than are single notes of music. What you take to be beauty or ugliness of sound is indeed nothing but beauty or ugliness of meaning. You are pleased by the sound of such words as gondola, vestments, chancel, ermine, manor-house. They seem to be fraught with a subtle onomatopoeia, severally suggesting by their sounds the grace or sanctity or solid comfort of the things which they connote. You murmur them luxuriously, dreamily. Prepare for a slight shock. Scrofula, investments, cancer, vermin, warehouse. Horrible words, are they not? But say gondola—scrofula, vestments—investments, and so on; and then lay your hand on your heart, and declare that the words in the first list are in mere sound nicer than the words in the second. Of course they are not. If gondola were a disease, and if a scrofula were a beautiful boat peculiar to a beautiful city, the effect of each word would be exactly the reverse of what it is. This rule may be applied to all the other words in the two lists. And these lists might, of course, be extended to infinity. The appropriately beautiful or ugly sound of any word is an illusion wrought on us by what the word connotes. Beauty sounds as ugly as ugliness sounds beautiful. Neither of them has by itself any quality in sound.

It follows, then, that the Christian names and surnames in my first class sound beautiful or ugly according to what they connote. The sound of those in the second class depends on the extent to which it suggests any known word more than another. Of course, there might be a name hideous in itself. There might, for example, be a Mr. Griggsbiggmiggs. But there is not. And the fact that I, after prolonged study of a Postal Directory, have been obliged to use my imagination as factory for a name that connotes nothing and is ugly in itself may be taken as proof that such names do not exist actually. You cannot stump me by citing Mr. Matthew Arnold's citation of the words 'Ragg is in custody,' and his comment that 'there was no Ragg by the Ilyssus.' 'Ragg' has not an ugly sound in itself. Mr. Arnold was jarred merely by its suggestion of something ugly, a rag, and by the cold brutality of the police-court reporter in withholding the prefix 'Miss' from a poor girl who had got into trouble. If 'Ragg' had been brought to his notice as the name of some illustrious old family, Mr. Arnold would never have dragged in the Ilyssus. The name would have had for him a savour of quaint distinction. The suggestion of a rag would never have struck him. For it is a fact that whatever thing may be connoted or suggested by a name is utterly overshadowed by the name's bearer (unless, as in the case of poor 'Ragg,' there is seen to be some connexion between the bearer and the thing implied by the name). Roughly, it may be said that all names connote their bearers, and them only.

To have a 'beautiful' name is no advantage. To have an 'ugly' name is no drawback. I am aware that this is a heresy. In a famous passage, Bulwer Lytton propounded through one of his characters a theory that 'it is not only the effect that the sound of a name has on others which is to be thoughtfully considered; the effect that his name produces on the man himself is perhaps still more important. Some names stimulate and encourage the owner, others deject and paralyse him.'

Bulwer himself, I doubt not, believed that there was something in this theory. It is natural that a novelist should. He is always at great pains to select for his every puppet a name that suggests to himself the character which he has ordained for that puppet. In real life a baby gets its surname by blind heredity, its other names by the blind whim of its parents, who know not at all what sort of a person it will eventually become. And yet, when these babies grow up, their names seem every whit as appropriate as do the names of the romantic puppets. 'Obviously,' thinks the novelist, 'these human beings must "grow to" their names; or else, we must be viewing them in the light of their names.' And the quiet ordinary people, who do not write novels, incline to his conjectures. How else can they explain the fact that every name seems to fit its bearer so exactly, to sum him or her up in a flash? The true explanation, missed by them, is that a name derives its whole quality from its bearer, even as does a word from its meaning. The late Sir Redvers Buller, tauredon hupoblepsas [spelled in Greek, from Plato's Phaedo 117b], was thought to be peculiarly well fitted with his name. Yet had it belonged not to him, but to (say) some gentle and thoughtful ecclesiastic, it would have seemed quite as inevitable. 'Gore' is quite as taurine as 'Buller,' and yet does it not seem to us the right name for the author of Lux Mundi? In connection with him, who is struck by its taurinity? What hint of ovinity would there have been for us if Sir Redvers' surname had happened to be that of him who wrote the Essays of Elia? Conversely, 'Charles Buller' seems to us now an impossible nom de vie for Elia; yet it would have done just as well, really. Even 'Redvers Buller' would have done just as well. 'Walter Pater' means for us—how perfectly!— the author of Marius the Epicurean, whilst the author of All Sorts and Conditions of Men was summed up for us, not less absolutely, in 'Walter Besant.' And yet, if the surnames of these two opposite Walters had been changed at birth, what difference would have been made? 'Walter Besant' would have signified a prose style sensuous in its severity, an exquisitely patient scholarship, an exquisitely sympathetic way of criticism. 'Walter Pater' would have signified no style, but an unslakable thirst for information, and a bustling human sympathy, and power of carrying things through. Or take two names often found in conjunction—Johnson and Boswell. Had the dear great oracle been named Boswell, and had the sitter-at-his-feet been named Johnson, would the two names seem to us less appropriate than they do? Should we suffer any greater loss than if Salmon were Gluckstein, and Gluckstein Salmon? Finally, take a case in which the same name was borne by two very different characters. What name could seem more descriptive of a certain illustrious Archbishop of Westminster than 'Manning'? It seems the very epitome of saintly astuteness. But for 'Cardinal' substitute 'Mrs.' as its prefix, and, presto! it is equally descriptive of that dreadful medio-Victorian murderess who in the dock of the Old Bailey wore a black satin gown, and thereby created against black satin a prejudice which has but lately died. In itself black satin is a beautiful thing. Yet for many years, by force of association, it was accounted loathsome. Conversely, one knows that many quite hideous fashions in costume have been set by beautiful women. Such instances of the subtle power of association will make clear to you how very easily a name (being neither beautiful nor hideous in itself) can be made hideous or beautiful by its bearer—how inevitably it becomes for us a symbol of its bearer's most salient qualities or defects, be they physical, moral, or intellectual.

Streets are not less characteristic than human beings. 'Look!' cried a friend of mine, whom lately I found studying a map of London, 'isn't it appalling? All these streets—thousands of them—in this tiny compass! Think of the miles and miles of drab monotony this map contains! I pointed out to him (it is a thinker's penalty to be always pointing things out to people) that his words were nonsense. I told him that the streets on this map were no more monotonous than the rivers on the map of England. Just as there were no two rivers alike, every one of them having its own speed, its own windings, depths, and shallows, its own way with the reeds and grasses, so had every street its own claim to an especial nymph, forasmuch as no two streets had exactly the same proportions, the same habitual traffic, the same type of shops or houses, the same inhabitants. In some cases, of course, the difference between the 'atmosphere' of two streets is a subtle difference. But it is always there, not less definite to any one who searches for it than the difference between (say) Hill Street and Pont Street, High Street Kensington and High Street Notting Hill, Fleet Street and the Strand. I have here purposely opposed to each other streets that have obvious points of likeness. But what a yawning gulf of difference is between each couple! Hill Street, with its staid distinction, and Pont Street, with its eager, pushful 'smartness,' its air de petit parvenu, its obvious delight in having been 'taken up'; High Street Notting Hill, down-at-heels and unashamed, with a placid smile on its broad ugly face, and High Street Kensington, with its traces of former beauty, and its air of neatness and self-respect, as befits one who in her day has been caressed by royalty; Fleet Street, that seething channel of business, and the Strand, that swollen river of business, on whose surface float so many aimless and unsightly objects. In every one of these thoroughfares my mood and my manner are differently affected. In Hill Street, instinctively, I walk very slowly—sometimes, even with a slight limp, as one recovering from an accident in the hunting-field. I feel very well-bred there, and, though not clever, very proud, and quick to resent any familiarity from those whom elsewhere I should regard as my equals. In Pont Street my demeanour is not so calm and measured. I feel less sure of myself, and adopt a slight swagger. In High Street, Kensington, I find myself dapper and respectable, with a timid leaning to the fine arts. In High Street, Notting Hill, I become frankly common. Fleet Street fills me with a conviction that if I don't make haste I shall be jeopardising the national welfare. The Strand utterly unmans me, leaving me with only two sensations: (1) a regret that I have made such a mess of my life; (2) a craving for alcohol. These are but a few instances. If I had time, I could show you that every street known to me in London has a definite effect on me, and that no two streets have exactly the same effect. For the most part, these effects differ in kind according only to the different districts and their different modes of life; but they differ in detail according to such specific little differences as exist between such cognate streets as

Bruton Street and Curzon Street, Doughty Street and Great Russell Street. Every one of my readers, doubtless, realises that he, too, is thus affected by the character of streets. And I doubt not that for him, as for me, the mere sound or sight of a street's name conjures up the sensation he feels when he passes through that street. For him, probably, the name of every street has hitherto seemed to be also its exact, inevitable symbol, a perfect suggestion of its character. He has believed that the grand or beautiful streets have grand or beautiful names, the mean or ugly streets mean or ugly names. Let me assure him that this is a delusion. The name of a street, as of a human being, derives its whole quality from its bearer.

'Oxford Street' sounds harsh and ugly. 'Manchester Street' sounds rather charming. Yet 'Oxford' sounds beautiful, and 'Manchester' sounds odious. 'Oxford' turns our thoughts to that 'adorable dreamer, whispering from her spires the last enchantments of the Middle Age.' An uproarious monster, belching from its factory-chimneys the latest exhalations of Hell—that is the image evoked by 'Manchester.' But neither in 'Manchester Street' is there for us any hint of that monster, nor in 'Oxford Street' of that dreamer. The names have become part and parcel of the streets. You see, then, that it matters not whether the name given to a new street be one which in itself suggests beauty, or one which suggests ugliness. In point of fact, it is generally the most pitiable little holes and corners that bear the most ambitiously beautiful names. To any one who has studied London, such a title as 'Paradise Court' conjures up a dark fetid alley, with untidy fat women gossiping in it, untidy thin women quarrelling across it, a host of haggard and shapeless children sprawling in its mud, and one or two drunken men propped against its walls. Thus, were there an official nomenclator of streets, he might be tempted to reject such names as in themselves signify anything beautiful. But his main principle would be to bestow whatever name first occurred to him, in order that he might save time for thinking about something that really mattered.

I have yet to fulfil the second part of my promise: show the futility of trying to commemorate a hero by making a street his namesake. By implication I have done this already. But, for the benefit of the less nimble among my readers, let me be explicit. Who, passing through the Cromwell Road, ever thinks of Cromwell, except by accident? What journalist ever thinks of Wellington in Wellington Street? In Marlborough Street, what policeman remembers Marlborough? In St. James's Street, has any one ever fancied he saw the ghost of a pilgrim wrapped in a cloak, leaning on a staff? Other ghosts are there in plenty. The phantom chariot of Lord Petersham dashes down the slope nightly. Nightly Mr. Ball Hughes appears in the bow-window of White's. At cock-crow Charles James Fox still emerges from Brooks's. Such men as these were indigenous to the street. Nothing will ever lay their ghosts there. But the ghost of St. James—what should it do in that galley?... Of all the streets that have been named after famous men, I know but one whose namesake is suggested by it. In Regent Street you do sometimes think of the Regent; and that is not because the street is named after him, but because it was conceived by him, and was designed and built under his auspices, and is redolent of his character and his time. When a national hero is to be commemorated by a street, he must be allowed to design the street himself. The mere plastering-up of his name is no mnemonic.

ON SHAKESPEARE'S BIRTHDAY

My florist has standing orders to deliver early on the morning of this day a chaplet of laurel. With it in my hand, I reach by a step-ladder the nobly arched embrasure that is above my central book-case, and crown there the marble brow of him whose name is the especial glory of our literature—of all literature. The greater part of the morning is spent by me in contemplation of that brow, and in silent meditation. And, year by year, always there intrudes itself into this meditation the hope that Shakespeare's name will, one day, be swept into oblivion.

I am not—you will have perceived that I certainly am not—a 'Baconian.' So far as I have examined the evidence in the controversy, I do not feel myself tempted to secede from the side on which (rightly, inasmuch as it is the obviously authoritative side) every ignorant person ranges himself. Even the hottest Baconian, filled with the stubbornest conviction, will, I fancy, admit in confidence that the utmost thing that could, at present, be said for his conclusions by a judicial investigator is that they are 'not proven.' To be convinced of a thing without being able to establish it is the surest recipe for making oneself ridiculous. The Baconians have thus made themselves very ridiculous; and that alone is reason enough for not wishing to join them. And yet my heart is with them, and my voice urges them to carry on the fight. It is a good fight, in my opinion, and I hope they will win it.

I do not at all understand the furious resentment they rouse in the bosoms of the majority. Mistaken they may be; but why yell them down as knavish blasphemers? Our reverence, after all, is given not to an Elizabethan named William Shakespeare, who was born at Stratford, and married, and migrated to London, and became a second-rate actor, and afterwards returned to Stratford, and made a will, and composed a few lines of doggerel for the tombstone under which he was buried. Our reverence is given to the writer of certain plays and sonnets. To that second-rate actor, because we believe he wrote those plays and sonnets, we give that reverence. But our belief is not such as we give to the proposition that one and two make three. It is a belief that has to be upheld by argument when it is assailed. When a man says to us that one and two make four, we smile and are silent. But when he argues, point by point, that in Bacon's life and writings there is nothing to show that Bacon might not have written the plays and sonnets, and that there is much to show that he did write them, and that in what we know about Shakespeare there is little evidence that Shakespeare wrote those works, and much evidence that he did not write them, then we pull ourselves together, marshalling all our facts and all out literary discernment, so as to convince our interlocutor of his error. But why should we not do our task urbanely? The cyphers, certainly, are stupid and tedious things, deserving no patience.

But the more intelligent Baconians spurn them as airily as do you or I. Our case is not so strong that the arguments of these gentlemen can be ignored; and naughty temper does but hamper us in the task of demolition. If Bacon were proved to have written Shakespeare's plays and sonnets, would mankind be robbed of one of those illusions which are necessary to its happiness and welfare? If so, we have a good excuse for browbeating the poor Baconians. But it isn't so, really and truly.

Suppose that one fine morning, Mr. Blank, an ardent Baconian, stumbled across some long-sought document which proved irrefragably that Bacon was the poet, and Shakespeare an impostor. What would be our sentiments? For the second-rate actor we should have not a moment's sneaking kindness or pity. On the other hand, should we not experience an everlasting thrill of pride and gladness in the thought that he who had been the mightiest of our philosophers had been also, by some unimaginable grace of heaven, the mightiest of our poets? Our pleasure in the plays and sonnets would be, of course, not one whit greater than it is now. But the pleasure of hero-worship for their author would be more than reduplicated. The Greeks revelled in reverence of Heracles by reason of his twelve labours. They would have been disappointed had it been proved to them that six of those labours had been performed by some quite obscure person. The divided reverence would have seemed tame. Conversely, it is pleasant to revere Bacon, as we do now, and to revere Shakespeare, as we do now; but a wildest ecstasy of worship were ours could we concentrate on one of those two demigods all that reverence which now we apportion to each apart.

It is for this reason, mainly, that I wish success to the Baconians. But there is another reason, less elevated perhaps, but not less strong for me. I should like to watch the multifarious comedies which would spring from the downfall of an idol to which for three centuries a whole world had been kneeling. Glad fancy makes for me a few extracts from the issue of a morning paper dated a week after the publication of Mr. Blank's discovery. This from a column of Literary Notes:

From Baiham, Sydenham, Lewisham, Clapham, Herne Hill and Peckham comes news that the local Shakespeare Societies have severally met and decided to dissolve. Other suburbs are expected to follow.

This from the same column:

Mr. Sidney Lee is now busily engaged on a revised edition of his monumental biography of Shakespeare. Yesterday His Majesty the King graciously visited Mr. Lee's library in order to personally inspect the progress of the work, which, in its complete form, is awaited with the deepest interest in all quarters.

And this, a leaderette:

Yesterday at a meeting of the Parks Committee of the London County Council it was unanimously resolved to recommend at the next meeting of the Council that the statue of Shakespeare in Leicester Square should be removed. This decision was arrived at in view of the fact that during the past few days the well-known effigy has been the centre of repeated disturbances, and is already considerably damaged. We are surprised to learn that there are in our midst persons capable of doing violence to a noble work of art merely because its subject is distasteful to them. But even the most civilised communities have their fits of vandalism. "Tis true, 'tis pity, and pity 'tis 'tis true.'

And this from a page of advertisements:

To be let or sold. A commodious and desirable Mansion at Stratford-on-Avon. Delightful flower and kitchen gardens. Hot and cold water on every floor. Within easy drive of station. Hitherto home of Miss Marie Corelli.

And this, again from the Literary Notes:

Mr. Hall Caine is in town. Yesterday, at the Authors' Club, he passed almost unrecognised by his many friends, for he has shaved his beard and moustache, and has had his hair cropped quite closely to the head. This measure he has taken, he says, owing to the unusually hot weather prevailing.

A sonnet, too, printed in large type on the middle page, entitled 'To Shakespeare,' signed by the latest fashionable poet, and beginning thus:

O undetected during so long years,
O irrepleviably infamous,
Stand forth!

A cable, too, from 'Our Own Correspondent' in New York:

This afternoon the Carmania came into harbour. Among the passengers was Mr. J. Pierpont Morgan, who had come over in personal charge of Anne Hathaway's Cottage, his purchase of which for L2,000,000 excited so much attention on your side a few weeks ago. Mr. Blank's sensational revelations not having been published to the world till two days after the Carmania left Liverpool, the millionaire collector had, of course, no cognisance of the same. On disembarking he proceeded straight to the Customs Office and inquired how much duty was to be imposed on the cottage. On being courteously informed that the article would be passed into the country free of charge, he evinced considerable surprise. I then ventured to approach Mr. Morgan and to hand him a journal containing the cabled summary of Mr. Blank's disclosures, which he proceeded to peruse. His comments I must reserve for the next mail, the cable clerks here demurring to their transmission.

Only a dream? But a sweet one. Bustle about, Baconians, and bring it true. Don't listen to my florist.

A HOME-COMING

Belike, returning from a long pilgrimage, in which you have seen many strange men and strange cities, and have had your imagination stirred by marvellous experiences, you have never, at the very end of your journey, almost in sight of your home, felt suddenly that all you had been seeing and learning was as naught—a pack of negligible illusions, faint and forgotten. From me, however, this queer sensation has not been withheld. It befell me a few days ago; in a cold grey dawn, and in the Buffet of Dover Harbour.

I had spent two months far away, wandering and wondering; and now I had just fulfilled two thirds of the little tripartite journey from Paris to London. I was sleepy, as one always is after that brief and twice broken slumber. I was chilly, for is not the dawn always bleak at Dover, and perforated always with a bleak and drizzling rain? I was sad, for I had watched from the deck the white cliffs of Albion coming nearer and nearer to me, towering over me, and in the familiar drizzle looking to me more than ever ghastly for that I had been so long and so far away from them. Often though that harsh, chalky coast had thus borne down on me, I had never yet felt so exactly and lamentably like a criminal arrested on an extradition warrant.

In its sleepy, chilly shell my soul was still shuddering and whimpering. Piteously it conjured me not to take it back into this cruel hum-drum. It rose up and fawned on me. 'Down, Sir, down!' said I sternly. I pointed out to it that needs must when the devil drives, and that it ought to think itself a very lucky soul for having had two happy, sunny months of fresh and curious adventure. 'A sorrow's crown of sorrow,' it murmured, 'is remembering happier things.' I declared the sentiment to be as untrue as was the quotation trite, and told my soul that I looked keenly forward to the pleasure of writing, in collaboration with it, that book of travel for which I had been so sedulously amassing notes and photographs by the way.

This colloquy was held at a table in the Buffet. I was sorry, for my soul's sake, to be sitting there. Britannia owns nothing more crudely and inalienably Britannic than her Buffets. The barmaids are but incarnations of her own self, thinly disguised. The stale buns and the stale sponge-cakes must have been baked, one fancies, by her own heavy hand. Of her everything is redolent. She it is that has cut the thick stale sandwiches, bottled the bitter beer, brewed the unpalatable coffee. Cold and hungry though I was, one sip of this coffee was one sip too much for me. I would not mortify my body by drinking more of it, although I had to mortify my soul by lingering over it till one of the harassed waiters would pause to be paid for it. I was somewhat comforted by the aspect of my fellow-travellers at the surrounding tables. Dank, dishevelled, dismal, they seemed to be resenting as much as I the return to the dear home-land. I suppose it was the contrast between them and him that made me stare so hard at the large young man who was standing on the threshold and surveying the scene.

He looked, as himself would undoubtedly have said, 'fit as a fiddle,' or 'right as rain.' His cheeks were rosy, his eyes sparkling. He had his arms akimbo, and his feet planted wide apart. His grey bowler rested on the back of his head, to display a sleek coating of hair plastered down over his brow. In his white satin tie shone a dubious but large diamond, and there was the counter-attraction of geraniums and maidenhair fern in his button-hole. So fresh was the nosegay that he must have kept it in water during the passage! Or perhaps these vegetables had absorbed by mere contact with his tweeds, the subtle secret of his own immarcescibility. I remembered now that I had seen him, without realising him, on the platform of the Gare du Nord. 'Gay Paree' was still written all over him. But evidently he was no repiner.

Unaccountable though he was, I had no suspicion of what he was about to do. I think you will hardly believe me when I tell you what he did. 'A traveller's tale' you will say, with a shrug. Yet I swear to you that it is the plain and solemn truth. If you still doubt me, you have the excuse that I myself hardly believed the evidence of my eyes. In the Buffet of Dover Harbour, in the cold grey dawn, in the brief interval between boat and train, the large young man, shooting his cuffs, strode forward, struck a confidential attitude across the counter, and began to flirt with the barmaid.

Open-mouthed, fascinated, appalled, I watched this monstrous and unimaginable procedure. I was not near enough to overhear what was said. But I knew by the respective attitudes that the time-honoured ritual was being observed strictly by both parties. I could see the ice of haughty indifference thawing, little by little, under the fire of gallant raillery. I could fix the exact moment when 'Indeed?' became 'I daresay,' and when 'Well, I must say' gave place to 'Go along,' and when 'Oh, I don't mind you—not particularly' was succeeded by 'Who gave you them flowers?'... All in the cold grey dawn...

The cry of 'Take your places, please!' startled me into realisation that all the other passengers had vanished. I hurried away, leaving the young man still in the traditional attitude which he had assumed from the first—one elbow sprawling on the counter, one foot cocked over the other. My porter had put my things into a compartment exactly opposite the door of the Buffet. I clambered in.

Just as the guard blew his whistle, the young man or monster came hurrying out. He winked at me. I did not return his wink.

I suppose I ought really to have raised my hat to him. Pre-eminently, he was one of those who have made England what it is. But they are the very men whom one does not care to meet just after long truancy in preferable lands. He was the backbone of the nation. But ought backbones to be exposed?

Though I would rather not have seen him then and there, I did realise, nevertheless, the overwhelming interest of him. I knew him to be a stranger sight, a more memorable and instructive, than any of the fair sights I had been seeing. He made them all seem nebulous and unreal to me. Beside me lay my despatch-box. I unlocked it, drew from it all the notes and all the photographs I had brought back with me. These, one by one, methodically, I tore up, throwing their fragments out of the window, not grudging them to the wind.

'THE RAGGED REGIMENT'

—'commonly called "Longshanks" on account of his great height he was the first king crowned in the Abbey as it now appears and was interred with great pomp on St. Simon's and St. Jude's Day October 28th 1307 in 1774 the tomb was opened when the king's body was found almost entire in the right hand was a richly embossed sceptre and in the left'—

So much I gather as I pass one of the tombs on my way to the Chapel of Abbot Islip. Anon the verger will have stepped briskly forward, drawing a deep breath, with his flock well to heel, and will be telling the secrets of the next tomb on his tragic beat.

To be a verger in Westminster Abbey—what life could be more unutterably tragic? We are, all of us, more or less enslaved to sameness; but not all of us are saying, every day, hour after hour, exactly the same thing, in exactly the same place, in exactly the same tone of voice, to people who hear it for the first time and receive it with a gasp of respectful interest. In the name of humanity, I suggest to the Dean and Chapter that they should relieve these sad-faced men of their intolerable mission, and purchase parrots. On every tomb, by every bust or statue, under every memorial window, let a parrot be chained by the ankle to a comfortable perch, therefrom to enlighten the rustic and the foreigner. There can be no objection on the ground of expense; for parrots live long. Vergers do not, I am sure.

It is only the rustic and the foreigner who go to Westminster Abbey for general enlightenment. If you pause beside any one of the verger-led groups, and analyse the murmur emitted whenever the verger has said his say, you will find the constituent parts of the sound to be such phrases as 'Lor!' 'Ach so!' 'Deary me!' 'Tiens!' and 'My!' 'My!' preponderates; for antiquities appeal with greatest force to the one race that has none of them; and it is ever the Americans who hang the most tenaciously, in the greatest numbers, on the vergers' tired lips. We of the elder races are capable of taking antiquities as a matter of course. Certainly, such of us as reside in London take Westminster Abbey as a matter of course. A few of us will be buried in it, but meanwhile we don't go to it, even as we don't go to the Tower, or the Mint, or the Monument. Only for some special purpose do we go—as to hear a sensational bishop preaching, or to see a monarch anointed. And on these rare occasions we cast but a casual glance at the Abbey—that close-packed chaos of beautiful things and worthless vulgar things. That the Abbey should be thus chaotic does not seem strange to us; for lack of orderliness and discrimination is an essential characteristic of the English genius. But to the Frenchman, with his passion for symmetry and harmony, how very strange it must all seem! How very whole-hearted a generalising 'Tiens! must he utter when he leaves the edifice!

My own special purpose in coming is to see certain old waxen effigies that are here. [In its original form this essay had the good fortune to accompany two very romantic drawings by William Nicholson—one of Queen Elizabeth's effigy, the other of Charles II.'s.] A key grates in the lock of a little door in the wall of (what I am told is) the North Ambulatory; and up a winding wooden staircase I am ushered into a tiny paven chamber. The light is dim, through the deeply embrased and narrow window, and the space is so obstructed that I must pick my way warily. All around are deep wooden cupboards, faced with glass; and I become dimly aware that through each glass some one is watching me. Like sentinels in sentry-boxes, they fix me with their eyes, seeming as though they would challenge me. How shall I account to them for my presence? I slip my note-book into my pocket, and try, in the dim light, to look as unlike a spy as possible. But I cannot, try as I will, acquit myself of impertinence. Who am I that I should review this 'ragged regiment'? Who am I that I should come peering in upon this secret conclave of the august dead? Immobile and dark, very gaunt and withered, these personages peer out at me with a malign dignity, through the ages which separate me from them, through the twilight in which I am so near to them. Their eyes... Come, sir, their eyes are made of glass. It is quite absurd to take wax-works seriously. Wax-works are not a serious form of art. The aim of art is so to imitate life as to produce in the spectator an illusion of life. Wax-works, at best, can produce no such illusion. Don't pretend to be illuded. For its power to illude, an art depends on its limitations. Art never can be life, but it may seem to be so if it do but keep far enough away from life. A statue may seem to live. A painting may seem to live. That is because each is so far away from life that you do not apply the test of life to it. A statue is of bronze or marble, than either of which nothing could be less flesh-like. A painting is a thing in two dimensions, whereas man is in three. If sculptor or painter tried to dodge these conventions, his labour would be undone. If a painter swelled his canvas out and in according to the convexities and concavities of his model, or if a sculptor overlaid his material with authentic flesh-tints, then you would demand that the painted or sculptured figure should blink, or stroke its chin, or kick its foot in the air. That it could do none of these things would rob it of all power to illude you. An art that challenges life at close quarters is defeated through the simple fact that it is not life. Wax-works, being so near to life, having the exact proportions of men and women, having the exact texture of skin and hair and habiliments, must either be made animate or continue to be grotesque and pitiful failures. Lifelike? They? Rather do they give you the illusion of death. They are akin to photographs seen through stereoscopic lenses— those photographs of persons who seem horribly to be corpses, or, at least, catalepts; and... You see, I have failed to cheer myself up. Having taken up a strong academic line, and set bravely out to prove to myself the absurdity of wax-works, I find myself at the point where I started, irrefutably arguing to myself that I have good reason to be frightened, here in the Chapel of Abbot Islip, in the midst of these, the Abbot's glowering and ghastly tenants. Catalepsy! death! that is the atmosphere I am breathing.

If I were writing in the past tense, I might pause here to consider whether this emotion was a genuine one or a mere figment for literary effect. As I am writing in the present tense, such a pause would be inartistic, and shall not be made. I must seem not to be writing, but to be actually on the spot, suffering. But then, you may well ask, why should I stay here, to suffer? why not beat a hasty retreat? The answer is that my essay would then seem skimpy; and that you, moreover, would know hardly anything about the wax-works. So I must ask you to imagine me fighting down my fears, and consoling myself with the reflection that here, after all, a sense of awe and oppression is just what one ought to feel—just what one comes for. At Madame Tussaud's exhibition, by which I was similarly afflicted some years ago, I had no such consolation. There my sense of fitness was outraged. The place was meant to be cheerful. It was brilliantly lit. A band was playing popular tunes. Downstairs there was even a restaurant. (Let fancy fondly dwell, for a moment, on the thought of a dinner at Madame Tussaud's: a few carefully-selected guests, and a menu well thought out; conversation becoming general; corks popping; quips flying; a sense of bien-etre; 'thank you for a most delightful evening.') Madame's figures were meant to be agreeable and lively presentments. Her visitors were meant to have a thoroughly good time. But the Islip Chapel has no cheerful intent. It is, indeed, a place set aside, with all reverence, to preserve certain relics of a grim, yet not unlovely, old custom. These fearful images are no stock-in-trade of a showman; we are not invited to 'walk-up' to them. They were fashioned with a solemn and wistful purpose. The reason of them lies in a sentiment which is as old as the world—lies in man's vain revolt from the prospect of death. If the soul must perish from the body, may not at least the body itself be preserved, somewhat in the semblance of life, and, for at least a while, on the face of the earth? By subtle art, with far-fetched spices, let the body survive its day and be (even though hidden beneath the earth) for ever. Nay more, since death cause it straightway to dwindle somewhat from the true semblance of life, let cunning artificers fashion it anew—fashion it as it was. Thus, in the earliest days of England, the kings, as they died, were embalmed, and their bodies were borne aloft upon their biers, to a sepulture long delayed after death. In later days, an image of every king that died was forthwith carved in wood, and painted according to his remembered aspect, and decked in his own robes; and, when they had sealed his tomb, the mourners, humouring, to the best of their power, his hatred of extinction, laid this image upon the tomb's slab, and left it so. In yet later days, the pretence became more realistic. The hands and the face were modelled in wax; and the figure stood upright, in some commanding posture, on a valanced platform above the tomb. Nor were only the kings thus honoured. Every one who was interred in the Abbey, whether in virtue of lineage or of achievements, was honoured thus. It was the fashion for every great lady to write in her will minute instructions as to the posture in which her image was to be modelled, and which of her gowns it was to be clad in, and with what of her jewellery it was to glitter. Men, too, used to indulge in such precautions. Of all the images thus erected in the Abbey, there remain but a few. The images had to take their chance, in days that were without benefit of police. Thieves, we may suppose, stripped the finery from many of them. Rebels, we know, broke in, less ignobly, and tore many of them limb from limb, as a protest against the governing classes. So only a poor remnant, a 'ragged regiment,' has been rallied, at length, into the sanctuary of Islip's Chapel. Perhaps, if they were not so few, these images would not be so fascinating.

Yes, I am fascinated by them now. Terror has been toned to wonder. I am filled with a kind of wondering pity. My academic theory about wax-works has broken down utterly. These figures—kings, princes, duchesses, queens— all are real to me now, and all are infinitely pathetic, in the dignity of their fallen and forgotten greatness. With what inalienable majesty they wear their rusty velvets and faded silks, flaunting sere ruffles of point-lace, which at a touch now would be shivered like cobwebs! My heart goes out to them through the glass that divides us. I wish I could stay with them, bear them company, always. I think they like me. I am afraid they will miss me. Perhaps it would be better for us never to have met. Even Queen Elizabeth, beholding whom, as she stands here, gaunt and imperious and appalling, I echo the words spoken by Philip's envoy, 'This woman is possessed of a hundred thousand devils'—even she herself, though she gazes askance into the air, seems to be conscious of my presence, and to be willing me to stay. It is a relief to meet the friendly bourgeois eye of good Queen Anne. It has restored my common sense. 'These figures really are most curious, most interesting...' and anon I am asking intelligent questions about the contents of a big press, which, by special favour, has been unlocked for me.

Perhaps the most romantic thing in the Islip Chapel is this press. Herein, huddled one against another in dark recesses, lie the battered and disjected remains of the earlier effigies—the primitive wooden ones. Edward I. and Eleanor are known to be among them; and Henry VII. and Elizabeth of York; and others not less illustrious. Which is which? By size and shape you can distinguish the men from the women; but beyond that is mere guesswork, be you never so expert. Time has broken and shuffled these erst so significant effigies till they have become as unmeaning for us as the bones in one of the old plague-pits. I feel that I ought to be more deeply moved than I am by this sad state of things. But I seem to have exhausted my capacity for sentiment; and I cannot rise to the level of my opportunity. Would that I were Thackeray! Dear gentleman, how promptly and copiously he would have wept and moralised here, in his grandest manner, with that perfect technical mastery which makes even now his tritest and shallowest sermons sound remarkable, his hollowest sentiment ring true! What a pity he never came to beat the muffled drum, on which he was so supreme a performer, around the Islip Chapel! As I make my way down the stairs, I am trying to imagine what would have been the cadence of the final sentence in this essay by Thackeray. And, as I pass along the North Ambulatory, lo! there is the same verger with a new party; and I catch the words 'was interred with great pomp on St. Simon's and St. Jude's Day October 28 1307 in 1774 the tomb was opened when—

THE HUMOUR OF THE PUBLIC

They often tell me that So-and-so has no sense of humour. Lack of this sense is everywhere held to be a horrid disgrace, nullifying any number of delightful qualities. Perhaps the most effective means of disparaging an enemy is to lay stress on his integrity, his erudition, his amiability, his courage, the fineness of his head, the grace of his figure, his strength of purpose, which has overleaped all obstacles, his goodness to his parents, the kind word that he has for every one, his musical voice, his freedom from aught that in human nature is base; and then to say what a pity it is that he has no sense of humour. The more highly you extol any one, the more eagerly will your audience accept anything you may have to say against him. Perfection is unloved in this imperfect world, but for imperfection comes instant sympathy. Any excuse is good enough for exalting the bad or stupid brother of us, but any stick is a valued weapon against him who has the effrontery to have been by Heaven better graced than we. And what could match for deadliness the imputation of being without sense of humour? To convict a man of that lack is to strike him with one blow to a level with the beasts of the field—to kick him, once and for all, outside the human pale. What is it that mainly distinguishes us from the brute creation? That we walk erect? Some brutes are bipeds. That we do not slay one another? We do. That we build houses? So do they. That we remember and reason? So, again, do they. That we converse? They are chatterboxes, whose lingo we are not sharp enough to master. On no possible point of superiority can we preen ourselves save this: that we can laugh, and that they, with one notable exception, cannot. They (so, at least, we assert) have no sense of humour. We have. Away with any one of us who hasn't!

Belief in the general humorousness of the human race is the more deep-rooted for that every man is certain that he himself is not without sense of humour. A man will admit cheerfully that he does not know one tune from another, or that he cannot discriminate the vintages of wines. The blind beggar does not seek to benumb sympathy by telling his patrons how well they are looking. The deaf and dumb do not scruple to converse in signals. 'Have you no sense of beauty?' I said to a friend who in the Accademia of Florence suggested that we had stood long enough in front of the 'Primavera.' 'No!' was his simple, straightforward, quite unanswerable answer. But I have never heard a man assert that he had no sense of humour. And I take it that no such assertion ever was made. Moreover, were it made, it would be a lie. Every man laughs. Frequently or infrequently, the corners of his mouth are drawn up into his cheeks, and through his parted lips comes his own particular variety, soft or loud, of that noise which is called laughter. Frequently or infrequently, every man is amused by something. Every man has a sense of humour, but not every man the same sense. A may be incapable of smiling at what has convulsed B, and B may stare blankly when he hears what has rolled A off his chair. Jokes are so diverse that no one man can see them all. The very fact that he can see one kind is proof positive that certain other kinds will be invisible to him. And so egoistic in his judgment is the average man that he is apt to suspect of being humourless any one whose sense of humour squares not with his own. But the suspicion is always false, incomparably useful though it is in the form of an accusation.

Having no love for the public, I have often accused that body of having no sense of humour. Conscience pricks me to atonement. Let me withdraw my oft-made imputation, and show its hollowness by examining with you, reader (who are, of course, no more a member of the public than I am), what are the main features of that sense of humour which the public does undoubtedly possess.

The word 'public' must, like all collective words, be used with caution. When we speak of our hair, we should remember not only that the hairs on our heads are all numbered, but also that there is a catalogue raisonne' in which every one of those hairs is shown to be in some respect unique. Similarly, let us not forget that 'public' denotes a collection not of identical units, but of units separable and (under close scrutiny) distinguishable one from another. I have said that not every man has the same sense of humour. I might have said truly that no two men have the same sense of humour, for that no two men have the same brain and heart and experience, by which things the sense of humour is formed and directed. One joke may go round the world, tickling myriads, but not two persons will be tickled in precisely the same way, to precisely the same degree. If the vibrations of inward or outward laughter could be (as some day, perhaps, they will be) scientifically registered, differences between them all would be made apparent to us. 'Oh,' is your cry, whenever you hear something that especially amuses you, 'I must tell that to' whomever you credit with a sense of humour most akin to your own. And the chances are that you will be disappointed by his reception of the joke. Either he will laugh less loudly than you hoped, or he will say something which reveals to you that it amuses him and you not in quite the same way. Or perhaps he will laugh so long and loudly that you are irritated by the suspicion that you have not yourself gauged the full beauty of it. In one of his books (I do not remember which, though they, too, I suppose, are all numbered) Mr. Andrew Lang tells a story that has always delighted and always will delight me. He was in a railway-carriage, and his travelling-companions were two strangers, two silent ladies, middle-aged. The train stopped at Nuneaton. The two ladies exchanged a glance. One of them sighed, and said, 'Poor Eliza! She had reason to remember Nuneaton!'... That is all. But how much! how deliciously and memorably much! How infinite a span of conjecture is in those dots which I have just made! And yet, would you believe me? some of my most intimate friends, the people most like to myself, see little or nothing of the loveliness of that pearl of price. Perhaps you would believe me. That is the worst of it: one never knows. The most sensitive intelligence cannot predict how will be appraised its any treasure by its how near soever kin.

This sentence, which I admit to be somewhat mannered, has the merit of bringing me straight to the point at which I have been aiming; that, though the public is composed of distinct units, it may roughly be regarded as a single entity. Precisely because you and I have sensitive intelligences, we cannot postulate certainly anything about each other. The higher an animal be in grade, the more numerous and recondite are the points in which its organism differs from that of its peers. The lower the grade, the more numerous and obvious the points of likeness. By 'the public' I mean that vast number of human animals who are in the lowest grade of intelligence. (Of course, this classification is made without reference to social 'classes.' The public is recruited from the upper, the middle, and the lower class. That the recruits come mostly from the lower class is because the lower class is still the least well-educated. That they come in as high proportion from the middle class as from the less well-educated upper class, is because the 'young Barbarians,' reared in a more gracious environment, often acquire a grace of mind which serves them as well as would mental keenness.) Whereas in the highest grade, to which you and I belong, the fact that a thing affects you in one way is no guarantee that it will not affect me in another, a thing which affects one man of the lowest grade in a particular way is likely to affect all the rest very similarly. The public's sense of humour may be regarded roughly as one collective sense.

It would be impossible for any one of us to define what are the things that amuse him. For him the wind of humour bloweth where it listeth. He finds his jokes in the unlikeliest places. Indeed, it is only there that he finds them at all. A thing that is labelled 'comic' chills his sense of humour instantly—perceptibly lengthens his face. A joke that has not a serious background, or some serious connexion, means nothing to him. Nothing to him, the crude jape of the professional jester. Nothing to him, the jangle of the bells in the wagged cap, the thud of the swung bladder. Nothing, the joke that hits him violently in the eye, or pricks him with a sharp point. The jokes that he loves are those quiet jokes which have no apparent point—the jokes which never can surrender their secret, and so can never pall. His humour is an indistinguishable part of his soul, and the things that stir it are indistinguishable from the world around him. But to the primitive and untutored public, humour is a harshly definite affair. The public can achieve no delicate process of discernment in humour. Unless a joke hits in the eye, drawing forth a shower of illuminative sparks, all is darkness. Unless a joke be labelled 'Comic. Come! why don't you laugh?' the public is quite silent. Violence and obviousness are thus the essential factors. The surest way of making a thing obvious is to provide it in some special place, at some special time. It is thus that humour is provided for the public, and thus that it is easy for the student to lay his hand on materials for an analysis of the public's sense of humour. The obviously right plan for the student is to visit the music-halls from time to time, and to buy the comic papers. Neither these halls nor these papers will amuse him directly through their art, but he will instruct himself quicklier and soundlier from them than from any other source, for they are the authentic sources of the public's laughter. Let him hasten to patronise them.

He will find that I have been there before him. The music-halls I have known for many years. I mean, of course, the real old-fashioned music-halls, not those depressing palaces where you see by grace of a biograph things that you have seen much better, and without a headache, in the street, and pitiable animals being forced to do things which Nature has forbidden them to do—things which we can do so very much better than they, without any trouble. Heaven defend me from those meaningless palaces! But the little old music-halls have always attracted me by their unpretentious raciness, their quaint monotony, the reality of the enjoyment on all those stolidly rapt faces in the audience. Without that monotony there would not be the same air of general enjoyment, the same constant guffaws. That monotony is the secret of the success of music-halls. It is not enough for the public to know that everything is meant to be funny, that laughter is craved for every point in every 'turn.' A new kind of humour, however obvious and violent, might take the public unawares, and be received in silence. The public prefers always that the old well-tested and well-seasoned jokes be cracked for it. Or rather, not the same old jokes, but jokes on the same old subjects. The quality of the joke is of slight import in comparison with its subject. It is the matter, rather than the treatment, that counts, in the art of the music-hall. Some subjects have come to be recognised as funny. Two or three of them crop up in every song, and before the close of the evening all of them will have cropped up many times. I speak with authority, as an earnest student of the music-halls. Of comic papers I know less. They have never allured me. They are not set to music—an art for whose cheaper and more primitive forms I have a very real sensibility; and I am not, as I peruse one of them, privy to the public's delight: my copy cannot be shared with me by hundreds of people whose mirth is wonderful to see and hear. And the bare contents are not such as to enchant me. However, for the purpose of this essay, I did go to a bookstall and buy as many of these papers as I could see—a terrific number, a terrific burden to stagger away with.

I have gone steadily through them, one by one. My main impression is of wonder and horror at the amount of hebdomadal labour implicit in them. Who writes for them? Who does the drawings for them—those thousands of little drawings, week by week, so neatly executed? To think that daily and nightly, in so many an English home, in a room sacred to the artist, sits a young man inventing and executing designs for Chippy Snips! To think how many a proud mother must be boasting to her friends: 'Yes, Edward is doing wonderfully well—more than fulfilling the hopes we always had of him. Did I tell you that the editor of Natty Tips has written asking him to contribute to his paper? I believe I have the letter on me. Yes, here it is,' etc., etc.! The awful thing is that many of the drawings in these comic papers are done with very real skill. Nothing is sadder than to see the hand of an artist wasted by alliance to a vacant mind, a common spirit. I look through these drawings, conceived all so tritely and stupidly, so hopelessly and helplessly, yet executed—many of them—so very well indeed, and I sigh over the haphazard way in which mankind is made. However, my concern is not with the tragedy of these draughtsmen, but with the specific forms taken by their humour. Some of them deal in a broad spirit with the world-comedy, limiting themselves to no set of funny subjects, finding inspiration in the habits and manners of men and women at large. 'HE WON HER' is the title appended to a picture of a young lady and gentleman seated in a drawing-room, and the libretto runs thus: 'Mabel: Last night I dreamt of a most beautiful woman. Harold: Rather a coincidence. I dreamt of you, too, last night.' I have selected this as a typical example of the larger style. This style, however, occupies but a small space in the bulk of the papers that lie before me. As in the music-halls, so in these papers, the entertainment consists almost entirely of variations on certain ever-recurring themes. I have been at pains to draw up a list of these themes. I think it is exhaustive. If any fellow-student detect an omission, let him communicate with me. Meanwhile, here is my list:—

Mothers-in-law
Hen-pecked husbands
Twins
Old maids
Jews
Frenchmen, Germans, Italians, Niggers (not Russians, or other foreigners of any denomination)
Fatness
Thinness
Long hair (worn by a man)
Baldness
Sea-sickness
Stuttering
Bad cheese

'Shooting the moon' (slang expression for leaving a lodging-house without paying the bill).

You might argue that one week's budget of comic papers is no real criterion—that the recurrence of these themes may be fortuitous. My answer to that objection is that this list coincides exactly with a list which (before studying these papers) I had made of the themes commonest, during the past few years, in the music-halls. This twin list, which results from separate study of the two chief forms of public entertainment, may be taken as a sure guide to the goal of our inquiry.

Let us try to find some unifying principle, or principles, among the variegated items. Take the first item—Mothers-in-law. Why should the public roar, as roar it does, at the mere mention of that relationship? There is nothing intrinsically absurd in the notion of a woman with a married daughter. It is probable that she will sympathise with her daughter in any quarrel that may arise between husband and wife. It is probable, also, that she will, as a mother, demand for her daughter more unselfish devotion than the daughter herself expects. But this does not make her ridiculous. The public laughs not at her, surely. It always respects a tyrant. It laughs at the implied concept of the oppressed son-in-law, who has to wage unequal warfare against two women. It is amused by the notion of his embarrassment. It is amused by suffering. This explanation covers, of course, the second item on my list—Hen-pecked husbands. It covers, also, the third and fourth items. The public is amused by the notion of a needy man put to double expense, and of a woman who has had no chance of fulfilling her destiny. The laughter at Jews, too, may be a survival of the old Jew-baiting spirit (though one would have thought that even the British public must have begun to realise, and to reflect gloomily, that the whirligig of time has so far revolved as to enable the Jews to bait the Gentiles). Or this laughter may be explained by the fact which alone can explain why the public laughs at Frenchmen, Germans, Italians, Niggers. Jews, after all, are foreigners, strangers. The British public has never got used to them, to their faces and tricks of speech. The only apparent reason why it laughs at the notion of Frenchmen, etc., is that they are unlike itself. (At the mention of Russians and other foreigners it does not laugh, because it has no idea what they are like: it has seen too few samples of them.)

So far, then, we have found two elements in the public's humour: delight in suffering, contempt for the unfamiliar. The former motive is the more potent. It accounts for the popularity of all these other items: extreme fatness, extreme thinness, baldness, sea-sickness, stuttering, and (as entailing distress for the landlady) 'shooting the moon.' The motive of contempt for the unfamiliar accounts for long hair (worn by a man). Remains one item unexplained. How can mirth possibly be evoked by the notion of bad cheese? Having racked my brains for the solution, I can but conjecture that it must be the mere ugliness of the thing. Why any one should be amused by mere ugliness I cannot conceive. Delight in cruelty, contempt for the unfamiliar, I can understand, though I cannot admire them. They are invariable elements in children's sense of humour, and it is natural that the public, as being unsophisticated, should laugh as children laugh. But any nurse will tell you that children are frightened by ugliness. Why, then, is the public amused by it? I know not. The laughter at bad cheese I abandon as a mystery. I pitch it among such other insoluble problems, as Why does the public laugh when an actor and actress in a quite serious play kiss each other? Why does it laugh when a meal is eaten on the stage? Why does it laugh when any actor has to say 'damn'?

If they cannot be solved soon, such problems never will be solved. For Mr. Forster's Act will soon have had time to make apparent its effects; and the public will proudly display a sense of humour as sophisticated as our own.

DULCEDO JUDICIORUM

When a 'sensational' case is being tried, the court is well filled by lay persons in need of a thrill. Their presence seems to be rather resented as a note of frivolity, a discord in the solemnity of the function, even a possible distraction for the judge and jury. I am not a lawyer, nor a professionally solemn person, and I cannot work myself up into a state of indignation against the interlopers. I am, indeed, one of them myself. And I am worse than one of them. I do not merely go to this or that court on this or that special occasion. I frequent the courts whenever I have nothing better to do. And it is rarely that, as one who cares to study his fellow-creatures, I have anything better to do. I greatly wonder that the courts are frequented by so few other people who have no special business there.

I can understand the glamour of the theatre. You find yourself in a queerly-shaped place, cut off from the world, with plenty of gilding and red velvet or blue satin. An orchestra plays tunes calculated to promote suppressed excitement. Presently up goes a curtain, revealing to you a mimic world, with ladies and gentlemen painted and padded to appear different from what they are. It is precisely the people most susceptible to the glamour of the theatre who are the greatest hindrances to serious dramatic art. They will stand anything, no matter how silly, in a theatre. Fortunately, there seems to be a decline in the number of people who are acutely susceptible to the theatre's glamour. I rather think the reason for this is that the theatre has been over-exploited by the press. Quite old people will describe to you their early playgoings with a sense of wonder, an enthusiasm, which—leaving a wide margin for the charm that past things must always have—will not be possible to us when we babble to our grandchildren. Quite young people, people ranging between the ages of four and five, who have seen but one or two pantomimes, still seem to have the glamour of the theatre full on them. But adolescents, and people in the prime of life, do merely, for the most part, grumble about the quality of the plays. Yet the plays of our time are somewhat better than the plays that were written for our elders. Certainly the glamour of the theatre has waned. And so much the better for the drama's future.

It is a matter of concern, that future, to me who have for so long a time been a dramatic critic. A man soon comes to care, quite unselfishly, about the welfare of the thing in which he has specialised. Of course, I care selfishly too. For, though it is just as easy for a critic to write interestingly about bad things as about good things, he would rather, for choice, be in contact with good things. It is always nice to combine business and pleasure. But one regrets, even then, the business. If I were a forensic critic, my delight in attending the courts would still be great; but less than it is in my irresponsibility. In the courts I find satisfied in me just those senses which in the theatre, nearly always, are starved. Nay, I find them satisfied more fully than they ever could be, at best, in any theatre. I do not merely fall back on the courts, in disgust of the theatre as it is. I love the courts better than the theatre as it ideally might be. And, I say again, I marvel that you leave me so much elbow-room there.

No artificial light is needed, no scraping of fiddles, to excite or charm me as I pass from the echoing corridor, through the swing-doors, into the well of this or that court. It matters not much to me what case I shall hear, so it be of the human kind, with a jury and with witnesses. I care little for Chancery cases. There is a certain intellectual pleasure in hearing a mass of facts subtly wrangled over. The mind derives therefrom something of the satisfaction that the eye has in watching acrobats in a music-hall. One wonders at the ingenuity, the agility, the perfect training. Like acrobats, these Chancery lawyers are a relief from the average troupe of actors and actresses, by reason of their exquisite alertness, their thorough mastery (seemingly exquisite and thorough, at any rate, to the dazzled layman). And they have a further advantage in their material. The facts they deal with are usually dull, but seldom so dull as facts become through the fancies of the average playwright. It is seldom that an evening in a theatre can be so pleasantly and profitably spent as a day in a Chancery court. But it is ever into one or another of the courts of King's Bench that I betake myself, for choice. Criminal trials, of which I have seen a few, I now eschew absolutely. I cannot stomach them. I know that it is necessary for the good of the community that such persons as infringe that community's laws should be punished. But, even were the mode of punishment less barbarous than it is, I should still prefer not to be brought in sight of a prisoner in the dock. Perhaps because I have not a strongly developed imagination, I have little or no public spirit. I cannot see the commonweal. On the other hand, I have plenty of personal feeling. And I have enough knowledge of men and women to know that very often the best people are guilty of the worst things. Is the prisoner in the dock guilty or not guilty of the offence with which he is charged? That is the question in the mind of the court. What sort of man is he? That is the question in my own mind. And the answer to the other question has no bearing whatsoever on the answer to this one. The English law assumes the prisoner innocent until he shall have been proved guilty. And, seeing him there a prisoner, a man who happens to have been caught, while others (myself included) are pleasantly at large after doing, unbeknown, innumerable deeds worse in the eyes of heaven than the deed with which this man is charged—deeds that do not prevent us from regarding our characters as quite fine really—I cannot but follow in my heart the example of the English law and assume (pending proof, which cannot be forthcoming) that the prisoner in the dock has a character at any rate as fine as my own. The war that this assumption wages in my breast against the fact that the man will perhaps be sentenced is too violent a war not to discommode me. Let justice be done. Or rather, let our rough-and-ready, well-meant endeavours towards justice go on being made. But I won't be there to see, thank you very much.

It is the natural wish of every writer to be liked by his readers. But how exasperating, how detestable, the writer who obviously touts for our affection, arranging himself for us in a mellow light, and inviting us, with gentle persistence, to note how lovable he is! Many essayists have made themselves quite impossible through their determination to remind us of Charles Lamb—'St. Charles,' as they invariably call him. And the foregoing paragraph, though not at all would-be-Lamb-like in expression, looks to me horribly like a blatant bid for your love. I hasten to add, therefore, that no absolutely kind-hearted person could bear, as I rejoice, to go and hear cases even in the civil courts. If it be true that the instinct of cruelty is at the root of our pleasure in theatrical drama, how much more is there of savagery in our going to look on at the throes of actual litigation—real men and women struggling not in make-believe, but in dreadful earnest! I mention this aspect merely as a corrective to what I had written. I do not pretend that I am ever conscious, as I enter a court, that I am come to gratify an evil instinct. I am but conscious of being glad to be there, on tiptoe of anticipation, whether it be to hear tried some particular case of whose matter I know already something, or to hear at hazard whatever case happen to be down for hearing. I never tire of the aspect of a court, the ways of a court. Familiarity does but spice them. I love the cold comfort of the pale oak panelling, the scurrying-in-and-out of lawyers' clerks, the eagerness and ominousness of it all, the rustle of silk as a K.C. edges his way to his seat and twists his head round for a quick whispered parley with his junior, while his client, at the solicitors' table, twists his head round to watch feverishly the quick mechanical nods of the great man's wig—the wig that covers the skull that contains the brain that so awfully much depends on. I love the mystery of those dark-green curtains behind the exalted Bench. One of them will anon be plucked aside, with a stentorian 'Silence!' Thereat up we jump, all of us as though worked by one spring; and in shuffles swiftly My Lord, in a robe well-fashioned for sitting in, but not for walking in anywhere except to a bathroom. He bows, and we bow; subsides, and we subside; and up jumps some grizzled junior—'My Lord, may I mention to your Lordship the case of "Brown v. Robinson and Another"?' It is music to me ever, the cadence of that formula. I watch the judge as he listens to the application, peering over his glasses with the lack-lustre eyes that judges have, eyes that stare dimly out through the mask of wax or parchment that judges wear. My Lord might be the mummy of some high tyrant revitalised after centuries of death and resuming now his sway over men. Impassive he sits, aloof and aloft, ramparted by his desk, ensconced between curtains to keep out the draught—for might not a puff of wind scatter the animated dust that he consists of? No creature of flesh and blood could impress us quite as he does, with a sense of puissance quite so dispassionate, so supernal. He crouches over us in such manner that we are all of us levelled one with another, shorn of aught that elsewhere differentiates us. The silk-gownsmen, as soon as he appears, fade to the semblance of juniors, of lawyers' clerks, of jurymen, of oneself. Always, indeed, in any public place devoted to some special purpose, one finds it hard to differentiate the visitors, hard to credit them with any private existence. Cast your eye around the tables of a cafe': how subtly similar all the people seem! How like a swarm of gregarious insects, in their unity of purpose and of aspect! Above all, how homeless! Cast your eye around the tables of a casino's gambling-room. What an uniform and abject herd, huddled together with one despondent impulse! Here and there, maybe, a person whom we know to be vastly rich; yet we cannot conceive his calm as not the calm of inward desperation; cannot conceive that he has anything to bless himself with except the roll of bank-notes that he has just produced from his breast-pocket. One and all, the players are levelled by the invisible presence of the goddess they are courting. Well, the visible presence of the judge in a court of law oppresses us with a yet keener sense of lowliness and obliteration. He crouches over us, visible symbol of the majesty of the law, and we wilt to nothingness beneath him. And when I say 'him' I include the whole judicial bench. Judges vary, no doubt. Some are young, others old, by the calendar. But the old ones have an air of physical incorruptibility—are 'well-preserved,' as by swathes and spices; and the young ones are just as mummified as they. Some of them are pleased to crack jokes; jokes of the sarcophagus, that twist our lips to obsequious laughter, but send a chill through our souls. There are 'strong' judges and weak ones (so barristers will tell you). Perhaps—who knows?—Minos was a strong judge, and Aeacus and Rhadamanthus were weak ones. But all three seem equally terrible to us. And so seem, in virtue of their position, and of the manner and aspect it invests them with, all the judges of our own high courts.

I hearken in awe to the toneless murmur in which My Lord comments on the application in the case of 'Brown v. Robinson and Another.' He says something about the Court of Crown Cases Reserved... Ah, what place on this earth bears a name so mystically majestic? Even in the commonest forensic phrases there is often this solemnity of cadence, always a quaintness, that stirs the imagination... The grizzled junior dares interject something 'with submission,' and is finally advised to see 'my learned brother in chambers.' 'As your Lordship pleases.'... We pass to the business of the day. I settle myself to enjoy the keenest form of aesthetic pleasure that is known to me.

Aesthetic, yes. In the law-courts one finds an art-form, as surely as in the theatre. What is drama? Its theme is the actions of certain opposed persons, historical or imagined, within a certain period of time; and these actions, these characters, must be shown to us in a succinct manner, must be so arranged that we know just what in them is essential to our understanding of them. Very similar is the art-form practised in the law-courts. The theme of a law-suit is the actions of certain actual opposed persons within a certain period of time; and these actions, these characters, must be set forth succinctly, in such-wise that we shall know just as much as is essential to our understanding of them. In drama, the presentment is, in a sense, more vivid. It is not—not usually, at least—retrospective. We see the actions being committed, hear the words as they are uttered. But how often do we have an illusion of their reality? Seldom. It is seldom that a masterpiece in drama is performed perfectly by an ideal cast. In a law-court, on the other hand, it is always in perfect form that the matter is presented to us. First the outline of the story, in the speech for the plaintiff; then this outline filled in by the examination of the plaintiff himself; then the other side of the story adumbrated by his cross-examination. Think of the various further stages of a law-suit, culminating in the judge's summing up; and you will agree with me that the whole thing is a perfect art-form. Drama, at its best, is clumsy, arbitrary, unsatisfying, by comparison. But what makes a law-suit the most fascinating, to me, of all art-forms, is that not merely its material, but the chief means of its expression, is life itself. Here, cited before us, are the actual figures in the actual story that has been told to us. Here they are, not as images to be evoked through the medium of printed page, or of painted canvas, or of disinterested ladies and gentlemen behind footlights. Actual, authentic, they stand before us, one by one, in the harsh light of day, to be made to reveal all that we need to know of them.

The most interesting witnesses, I admit, are they who are determined not to accommodate us—not to reveal themselves as they are, but to make us suppose them something quite different. All witnesses are more or less interesting. As I have suggested, there is no such thing as a dull law-suit. Nothing that has happened is negligible. And, even so, every human being repays attention—especially so when he stands forth on his oath. The strangeness of his position, and his consciousness of it, suffice in themselves to make him interesting. But it is disingenuousness that makes him delightful. And the greatest of all delights that a law-court can give us is a disingenuous witness who is quick-minded, resourceful, thoroughly master of himself and his story, pitted against a counsel as well endowed as himself. The most vivid and precious of my memories is of a case in which a gentleman, now dead, was sued for breach of promise, and was cross-examined throughout a whole hot day in midsummer by the late Mr. Candy. The lady had averred that she had known him for many years. She called various witnesses, who testified to having seen him repeatedly in her company. She produced stacks of letters in a handwriting which no expert could distinguish from his. The defence was that these letters were written by the defendant's secretary, a man who was able to imitate exactly his employer's handwriting, and who was, moreover, physically a replica of his employer. He was dead now; and the defendant, though he was a very well-known man, with many friends, was unable to adduce any one who had seen that secretary dead or alive. Not a soul in court believed the story. As it was a complicated story, extending over many years, to demolish it seemed child's play. Mr. Candy was no child. His performance was masterly. But it was not so masterly as the defendant's; and the suit was dismissed. In the light of common sense, the defendant hadn't a leg to stand on. Technically, his case was proved. I doubt whether I shall ever have a day of such acute mental enjoyment as was the day of that cross-examination.

I suppose that the most famous cross-examination in our day was Sir Charles Russell's of Pigott. It outstands by reason of the magnitude of the issue, and the flight and suicide of the witness. Had Pigott been of the stuff to stand up to Russell, and make a fight of it, I should regret far more keenly than I do that I was not in court. As it is, my regret is keen enough. I was reading again, only the other day, the verbatim report of Pigott's evidence, in one of the series of little paper volumes published by The Times; and I was revelling again in the large perfection with which Russell accomplished his too easy task. Especially was I amazed to find how vividly Russell, as I remember him, lived again, and could be seen and heard, through the medium of that little paper volume. It was not merely as though I had been in court, and were now recalling the inflections of that deep, intimidating voice, the steadfast gaze of those dark, intimidating eyes, and were remembering just at what points the snuff-box was produced, and just how long the pause was before the pinch was taken and the bandana came into play. It was almost as though these effects were proceeding before my very eyes—these sublime effects of the finest actor I have ever seen. Expressed through a perfect technique, his personality was overwhelming. 'Come, Mr. Pigott,' he is reported as saying, at a crucial moment, 'try to do yourself justice. Remember! you are face to face with My Lords.' How well do I hear, in that awful hortation, Russell's pause after the word 'remember,' and the lowered voice in which the subsequent words were uttered slowly, and the richness of solemnity that was given to the last word of all, ere the thin lips snapped together—those lips that were so small, yet so significant, a feature of that large, white, luminous and inauspicious face. It is an hortation which, by whomsoever delivered, would tend to dispirit the bravest and most honest of witnesses. The presence of a judge is always, as I have said, oppressive. The presence of three is trebly so. Yet not a score of them serried along the bench could have outdone in oppressiveness Sir Charles Russell. He alone, among the counsel I have seen, was an exception to the rule that by a judge every one in court is levelled. On the bench, in his last years, he was not notably more predominant than he ever had been. And the reason of his predominance at the Bar was not so much in the fact that he had no rival in swiftness, in subtlety, in grasp, as in the passionate strength of his nature, the intensity that in him was at the root of the grand manner.

In the courts, as in parliament and in the theatre, the grand manner is a thing of the past. Mr. Lloyd-George is not, in style and method, more remote from Gladstone, nor Mr. George Alexander from Macready, than is Mr. Rufus Isaacs, the type of modern advocate, from Russell. Strength, passion, sonorousness, magnificence of phrasing, are things which the present generation vaguely approves in retrospect; but it would titter at a contemporary demonstration of them. While I was reading Pigott's cross-examination, an idea struck me; why do not the managers of our theatres, always querulous about the dearth of plays, fall back on scenes from famous trials? A trial-scene in a play, though usually absurd, is almost always popular. Why not give us actual trial-scenes? They could not, of course, be nearly so exciting as the originals, for the simple reason that they would not be real; but they would certainly be more exciting than the average play. Thus I mused, hopefully. But I was brought up sharp by the reflection that it were hopeless to look for an actor who could impersonate Russell—could fit his manner to Russell's words, or indeed to the words of any of those orotund advocates. To reproduce recent trials would be a hardly warrantable thing. The actual participators in them would have a right to object (delighted though many of them would be). Vain, then, is my dream of theatres invigorated by the leavings of the law-courts. On the other hand, for the profit of the law-courts, I have a quite practicable notion. They provide the finest amusement in London, for nothing. Why for nothing? Let some scale of prices for admission be drawn up—half-a-guinea, say, for a seat in the well of the court, a shilling for a seat in the gallery, five pounds for a seat on the bench. Then, I dare swear, people would begin to realise how fine the amusement is.

WORDS FOR PICTURES

'HARLEQUIN'

A SIGN-BOARD, PAINTED ON COPPER, SIGNED 'W. EVANS, LONDON' CIRCA 1820

Harlequin dances, and, over the park he dances in, surely there is thunder brooding. His figure stands out, bright, large, and fantastic. But all around him is sultry twilight, and the clouds, pregnant with thunder, lower over him as he dances, and the elms are dim with unusual shadow. There is a tiny river in the dim distance. Under one of the nearest elms you may descry a square tomb, topped with an urn. What lord or lady underlies it? I know not. Harlequin dances. Sheathed in his gay suit of red and green and yellow lozenges, he ambles lightly over the gravel. At his feet lie a tambourine and a mask. Brown ferns fringe his pathway. With one hand he clasps the baton to his hip, with the other he points mischievously to his forehead. He wears a flat, loose cap of yellow. There is a ruff about his neck, and a pair of fine buckles to his shoes, and he always dances. He has his back to the thunderclouds, but there is that in his eyes which tells us that he has seen them, and that he knows their presage. He is afraid. Yet he dances. Never, howsoever slightly, swerves he, see! from his right posture, nor fail his feet in their pirouette. All a' merveille! Nor fades the smile from his face, though he smiles through the tarnished air of a sultry twilight, under the shadow of impending storm.

'THE GARDEN OF LOVE'
A PAINTING BY RUBENS, IN THE PRADO

Here they are met.

Here, by the balustrade, these lords and lusty ladies are met to romp and wanton in the fulness of love, under the solstice of a noon in midsummer. Water gushes in fantastic arcs from the grotto, making a cold music to the emblazoned air, while a breeze swells the sun-shot satin of every lady's skirt, and tosses the ringlets that hang like bunches of yellow grapes on either side of her brow, and stirs the plumes of her gallant. But the very breeze is laden with heat, and the fountain's noise does but whet the thirst of the grass, the flowers, the trees. The earth sulks under the burden of the unmerciful sun. Love itself, one had said, would be languid here, pale and supine, and, faintly sighing for things past or for future things, would sink into siesta. But behold! these are no ordinary lovers. The gushing fountains are likelier to run dry there in the grotto than they to falter in their redundant energy. These sanguine lords and ladies crave not an instant's surcease. They are tyrants and termagants of love.

If they are thus at noon, here under the sun's rays, what, one wonders, must be their manner in the banqueting hall, when the tapers gleam adown the long tables, and the fruits are stripped of their rinds, and the wine brims over the goblets, all to the music of the viols? Somehow, one cannot imagine them anywhere but in this sunlight. To it they belong. They are creatures of Nature, pagans untamed, lawless and unabashed. For all they are robed in crimson and saffron, and are with such fine pearls necklaced, these dames do exhale from their exuberant bodies the essence of a quite primitive and simple era; but for the ease of their deportment in their frippery, they might be Maenads in masquerade. They have nothing of the coyness that civilisation fosters in women, are as fearless and unsophisticated as men. A 'wooing' were wasted on them, for they have no sense of antagonism, and seek not by any means to elude men. They meet men even as rivers meet the sea. Even as, when fresh water meets salt water in the estuary, the two tides revolve in eddies and leap up in foam, so do these men and women laugh and wrestle in the rapture of concurrence. How different from the first embrace which marks the close of a wooing! that moment when the man seeks to conceal his triumph under a semblance of humility, and the woman her humiliation under a pretty air of patronage. Here, in the Garden of Love, they have none of those spiritual reservations and pretences. Nor is here any savour of fine romance. Nothing is here but the joy of satisfying a physical instinct—a joy that expresses itself not in any exaltation of words or thoughts, but in mere romping. See! Some of the women are chasing one another through the grotto. They are rushing headlong under the fountain. What though their finery be soaked? Anon they will come out and throw themselves on the grass, and the sun will quickly dry them.

Leave them, then, to their riot. Look upon these others who sit and stand here in a voluptuous bevy, hand in hand under the brazen sun, or flaunt to and fro, lolling in one another's arms and laughing in one another's faces. And see how closely above them hover the winged loves! One, upside down in the air, sprinkles them with rose-leaves; another waves over them a blazing torch; another tries to frighten them with his unarrowed bow. Another yet has dared to descend into the group; he nestles his fat cheek on a lady's lap, and is not rebuked. These little chubby Cythareans know they are privileged to play any pranks here. Doubtless they love to be on duty in this garden, for here they are patted and petted, and have no real work to do. At close of day, when they fly back to their mother, there is never an unmated name in the report they bring her; and she, belike, being pleased with them, allows them to sit up late, and to have each a slice of ambrosia and a sip of nectar. But elsewhere they have hard work, and often fly back in dread of Venus' anger. At that other balustrade, where Watteau, remembering this one, painted for us the 'Plaisirs du Bal,' how often they have lain in ambush, knowing that were one of them to show but the tip of his wings those sedate and migniard masqueraders would faint for very shame; yet ever hoping that they might, by their unseen presence, turn that punctilio of flirtation into love. And always they have flown back from Dulwich unrequited for all the pains they had taken, and pouting that Venus should ever send them on so hard an errand. But a day in this garden is always for them a dear holiday. They live in dread lest Venus discover how superfluous they are here. And so, knowing that the hypocrite's first dupe must be himself, they are always pretending to themselves that they are of some use. See that child yonder, perched on the balustrade, reading aloud from a scroll the praise of love as earnestly as though his congregation were of infidels. And that other, to the side, pushing two lovers along as though they were the veriest laggarts. The torch-bearer, too, and the archer, and the sprinkler of the rose-leaves—they are all, after their kind, trying to persuade themselves that they are needed. All but he who leans over and nestles his fat cheek on a lady's lap, as fondly and confidingly as though she were his mother... And truly, the lady is very like his mother. So, indeed, are all the other ladies. Strange! In all their faces is an uniformity of divine splendour. Can it be that Venus, impatient of mere sequences of lovers, has obtained leave of Jove to multiply herself, and that to-day by a wild coincidence her every incarnation has trysted an adorer to this same garden? Look closely! It must be so...

Hush! Let us keep her secret.

'ARIANE ET DIONYSE'
A PAINTING BY PAUL BERGERON, 1740

PAUVRETTE! no wonder she is startled. All came on her so suddenly. A moment since, she was alone on this island. Theseus had left her. Her lover had crept from her couch as she lay sleeping, and had sailed away with his comrades, noiselessly, before the sun rose and woke her.

From the top of yonder hillock she had seen the last sail of his argosy fading over the sea-line. Vainly she had waved her arms, and vainly her cries had echoed through all the island. She had run distraught through the valleys, the goats scampering before her to their own rocks. She had strayed, wildly weeping, along the shore, and the very sky had seemed to mock her. At length, spent with sorrow and wan with her tears, she had lain upon the sand. Above her the cliff sloped gently down to the shore, and all around her was the hot noontide, and no sound save the rustling of the sea over the sand. Theseus had left her. The sea had taken him from her. Let the sea take her in its tide.... Suddenly—what was that?—she leapt up and listened. Voices, voices, the loud clash of cymbals! She looked round for some place to hide in. Too late! Some man (goat or man) came bounding towards her down the cliff. Another came after him. Then others, a whole company, and with them many naked, abominable women, laughing and shrieking and waving leafy wands, as they rushed down towards her. And in their midst, in a brazen chariot drawn by panthers, sped one whose yellow hair streamed far behind him in the wind. And from his chariot he sprang and stood before her.

But she shrinks from his smile. She shrinks from the riot and ribaldry that encompass her. She is but a young bride whom the bridegroom has betrayed, and she would fain be alone in the bitterness of her anguish and her humiliation. Why have they come, these creatures who are stamping and reeling round her, these flushed women who clap the cymbals, and these wild men with the hoofs and the horns of goats? How should they comfort her? She is not of their race; no! nor even of their time. She stands among them, just as Bergeron saw her, a delicate, timid figurine du dix-huitie'me sie'cle. With her powdered hair and her hooped skirt and her stiff bodice of rose silk, she seems more fit for the consolations of some old Monsignore than for the homage of these frenzied Pagans and the amorous regard of their master. At him, pressing her shut fan to her lips, she is gazing across her shoulder. With one hand she seems to ward him from her. Her whole body is bent to flight, but she is 'affear'd of her own feet.' She is well enough educated to know that he who smiles at her is no mortal, but Bacchus himself, the very lord of Naxos. He stands before her, the divine debauchee racemiferis frontem circumdatus uvis; and all around her, a waif on his territory, are the symbols of his majesty and his power. It is in his honour that the ivy trails down the cliff, and are not the yews and the firs and the fig-trees that overshadow the cliff's edge all sacred to him? and the vines beyond, are they not all his? His four panthers are clawing the sand, and four tipsy Satyrs hold them, the impatient beasts, by their bridles. Another Satyr drags to execution a goat that he has caught cropping the vine; and in his slanted eyes one can see thirst for the blood of his poor cousin. The Maenads are dancing in one another's arms, and their tresses are coiled and crowned with tiny serpents. One of them kneels apart, sucking a great wine-skin. And yonder, that old cupster, Silenus, that horrible old favourite, wobbles along on a donkey, and would tumble off, you may be sure, were he not upheld by two fairly sober Satyrs. But the eyes of Ariadne are fixed only on the smooth-faced god. See how he smiles back at her with that lascivious condescension which is all that a god's love can be for a mortal girl! In his hand he holds a long thyrsus. Behind him is borne aloft a chaplet of seven gold stars.

Ariadne is but a little waif in the god's power. Not Theseus himself could protect her. One tap of the god's wand, and, lo! she, too, would be filled with the frenzy of worship, and, with a wild cry, would join the dancers, his for ever. But the god is not unscrupulous. He would fain win her by gentle and fair means, even by wedlock. That chaplet of seven stars is his bridal offering. Why should not she accept it? Why should she be coy of his desire? It is true that he drinks. But in time, may be, a wife might be able to wean him from the wine-skin, and from the low company he affects. That will be for time to show. And, meanwhile, how brilliant a match! Not even Pasiphae, her mother, ever contemplated for her such splendour. In her great love, Ariadne risked her whole future by eloping with Theseus. For her—the daughter of a far mightier king than Aegeus, and, on the distaff side, the granddaughter of Apollo—even marriage with Theseus would have been a me'salliance. And now, here is a chance, a chance most marvellous, of covering her silly escapade. She will be sensible, I think, though she is still a little frightened. She will accept this god's suit, if only to pique Theseus—Theseus, who, for all his long, tedious anecdotes of how he slew Procrustes and the bull of Marathon and the sow of Cromyon, would even now lie slain or starving in her father's labyrinth, had she not taken pity on him. Yes, it was pity she felt for him. She never loved him. And then, to think that he, a mere mortal, dared to cast her off—oh, it is too absurd, it is too monstrous!

'PETER THE DOMINICAN'
A PAINTING BY GIOVANNI BELLINI, IN THE NATIONAL GALLERY

'Credo in Dominum' were the words this monk wrote in the dust of the high-road, as he lay a-dying there of Cavina's dagger; and they, according to the Dominican record, were presently washed away by his own blood—'rapida profusio sui sanguinis delevit professionem suoe fidei.' Yet they had not been written in vain. On Cavina himself their impression was less delible, for did he not submit himself to the Church, and was he not, after absolution, received into that monastery which his own victim had founded? Here, before this picture by Bellini, one looks instinctively for the three words in the dust. They are not yet written there; for scarcely, indeed, has the dagger been planted in the Saint's breast. But here, to the right, on this little scroll of parchment that hangs from a fence of osiers, there are some words written, and one stoops to decipher them... JOANNES BELLINUS FECIT.

Now, had the Saint and his brother Dominican not been waylaid on their journey, they would have passed by this very fence, and would have stooped, as we do, to decipher the scroll, and would have very much wondered who was Bellinus, and what it was that he had done. The woodmen and the shepherd in the olive-grove by the roadside, the cowherds by the well, yonder—they have seen the scroll, I dare say, but they are not scholars enough to have read its letters. Cavina and his comrade in arms, lying in wait here, probably did not observe it, so intent were they for that pious and terrible Inquisitor who was to pass by. How their hearts must have leapt when they saw him, at length, with his companion, coming across that little arched bridge from the town—a conspicuous, unmistakable figure, clad in the pied frock of his brotherhood and wearing the familiar halo above his closely-shorn pate.

Cavina stands now over the fallen Saint, planting the short dagger in his heart. The other Dominican is being chased by Cavina's comrade, his face wreathed in a bland smile, his hands stretched childishly before him. Evidently he is quite unconscious how grave his situation is. He seems to think that this pursuit is merely a game, and that if he touch the wood of the olive-trees first, he will have won, and that then it will be his turn to run after this man in the helmet. Or does he know perhaps that this is but a painting, and that his pursuer will never be able to strike him, though the chase be kept up for many centuries? In any case, his smile is not at all seemly or dramatic. And even more extraordinary is the behaviour of the woodmen and the shepherd and the cowherds. Murder is being done within a yard or two of them, and they pay absolutely no attention. How Tacitus would have delighted in this example of the 'inertia rusticorum'! It is a great mistake to imagine that dwellers in quiet districts are more easily excited by any event than are dwellers in packed cities. On the contrary, the very absence of 'sensations' produces an atrophy of the senses. It is the constant supply of 'sensations' which creates a real demand for them in cities. Suppose that in our day some specially unpopular clergyman were martyred 'at the corner of Fenchurch Street,' how the 'same old crush' would be intensified! But here, in this quiet glade 'twixt Milan and Como, on this quiet, sun-steeped afternoon in early Spring, with a horrible outrage being committed under their very eyes, these callous clowns pursue their absurd avocations, without so much as resting for one moment to see what is going on.

Cavina plants the dagger methodically, and the Inquisitor himself is evidently filled with that intense self-consciousness which sustains all martyrs in their supreme hour and makes them, it may be, insensible to actual pain. One feels that this martyr will write his motto in the dust with a firm hand. His whole comportment is quite exemplary. What irony that he should be unobserved! Even we, posterity, think far less of St. Peter than of Bellini when we see this picture; St. Peter is no more to us than the blue harmony of those little hills beyond, or than that little sparrow perched on a twig in the foreground. After all, there have been so many martyrs—and so many martyrs named Peter—but so few great painters. The little screed on the fence is no mere vain anachronism. It is a sly, rather malicious symbol. PERIIT PETRUS: BILLINUS FECIT, as who should say.

'L'OISEAU BLEU'
A PAINTING ON SILK BY CHARLES CONDER

Over them, ever over them, floats the Blue Bird; and they, the ennuye'es and the ennuyants, the ennuyantes and the ennuye's, these Parisians of 1830, are lolling in a charmed, charming circle, whilst two of their order, the young Duc de Belhabit et Profil-Perdu with the girl to whom he has but recently been married, move hither or thither vaguely, their faces upturned, making vain efforts to lure down the elusive creature. The haze of very early morning pervades the garden which is the scene of their faint aspiration. One cannot see very clearly there. The ladies' furbelows are blurred against the foliage, and the lilac-bushes loom through the air as though they were white clouds full of rain. One cannot see the ladies' faces very clearly. One guesses them, though, to be supercilious and smiling, all with the curved lips and the raised eyebrows of Experience. For, in their time, all these ladies, and all their lovers with them, have tried to catch this same Blue Bird, and have been full of hope that it would come fluttering down to them at last. Now they are tired of trying, knowing that to try were foolish and of no avail. Yet it is pleasant for them to see, as here, others intent on the old pastime. Perhaps—who knows?—some day the bird will be trapped... Ah, look! Monsieur Le Duc almost touched its wing! Well for him, after all, that he did not more than that! Had he caught it and caged it, and hung the gilt cage in the boudoir of Madame la Duchesse, doubtless the bird would have turned out to be but a moping, drooping, moulting creature, with not a song to its little throat; doubtless the blue colour is but dye, and would soon have faded from wings and breast. And see! Madame la Duchesse looks a shade fatigued. She must not exert herself too much. Also, the magic hour is all but over. Soon there will be sunbeams to dispel the dawn's vapour; and the Blue Bird, with the sun sparkling on its wings, will have soared away out of sight. Allons! The little rogue is still at large.

'MACBETH AND THE WITCHES'
A PAINTING BY COROT, IN THE HERTFORD
HOUSE COLLECTION

Look! Across the plain yonder, those three figures, dark and gaunt against the sky.... Who are they? What are they? One of them is pointing with rigid arm towards the gnarled trees that from the hillside stretch out their storm-broken boughs and ragged leaves against the sky. Shifting thither, my eye discerns through the shadows two horsemen, riding slowly down the incline. Hush! I hold up a warning finger to my companion, lest he move. On what strange and secret tryst have we stumbled? They must not know they are observed. Could we creep closer up to them? Nay, the plain is so silent: they would hear us; and so barren: they would surely see us. Here, under cover of this rock, we can crouch and watch them.... We discern now more clearly those three expectants. One of them has a cloak of faded blue; it is fluttering in the wind. Women or men are they? Scarcely human they seem: inauspicious beings from some world of shadows, magically arisen through that platform of broken rock whereon they stand. The air around, even the fair sky above, is fraught by them with I know not what of subtle bale. One would say they had been waiting here for many days, motionless, eager but not impatient, knowing that at this hour the two horsemen would come. And we—it is strange—have we not ere now beheld them waiting? In some waking dream, surely, we have seen them, and now dimly recognise them. And the two horsemen, forcing their steeds down the slope—them, too, we have seen, even so. The light through a break in the trees faintly reveals them to us. They are accoutred in black armour. They seem not to be yet aware of the weird figures confronting them across the plain. But the horses, with some sharper instinct, are aware and afraid, straining, quivering. One of them throws back its head, but dares not whinny. As though under some evil spell, all nature seems to be holding its breath. Stealthily, noiselessly, I turn the leaves of my catalogue... 'Macbeth and the Witches.' Why, of course!

Of the two horsemen, which is Macbeth, which Banquo? Though we peer intently, we cannot in those distant shadows distinguish which is he that shall be king hereafter, which is he that shall merely beget kings. It is mainly in virtue of this very vagueness and mystery of manner that the picture is so impressive. An illustration should stir our fancy, leaving it scope and freedom. Most illustrations, being definite, do but affront us. Usually, Shakespeare is illustrated by some Englishman overawed by the poet's repute, and incapable of treating him, as did Corot, vaguely and offhand. Shakespeare expressed himself through human and superhuman characters; therefore in England none but a painter of figures would dare illustrate him. Had Corot been an Englishman, this landscape would have had nothing to do with Shakespeare. Luckily, as an alien, he was untrammelled by piety to the poet. He could turn Shakespeare to his own account. In this picture, obviously, he was creating, and only in a secondary sense illustrating. For him the landscape was the thing. Indeed, the five little figures may have been inserted by him as an afterthought, to point and balance the composition. Vaguely he remembered hearing of Macbeth, or reading it in some translation. Ce Sac-espe're...un beau talent...ne' romantique. Hugo he would not have attempted to illustrate. But Sac-espe're—why not? And so the little figures came upon the canvas, dim sketches. Charles Lamb disliked theatrical productions of Shakespeare's plays, because of the constraint thus laid on his imagination. But in the theatre, at least, we are diverted by movement, recompensed by the sound of the poet's words and (may be) by human intelligence interpreting his thoughts; whereas from a definite painting of Shakespearean figures we get nothing but an equivalent for the mimes' appearance: nothing but the painter's bare notion (probably quite incongruous with our notion) of what these figures ought to look like. Take Macbeth as an instance. From a definite painting of him what do we get? At worst, the impression of a kilted man with a red beard and red knees, brandishing a claymore. At best, a sombre barbarian doing nothing in particular. In either case, all the atmosphere, all the character, all the poetry, all that makes Macbeth live for us, is lost utterly. If these definite illustrations of Shakespeare's human figures affront us, how much worse is it when an artist tries his hand at the figures that are superhuman! Imagine an English illustrator's projection of the weird sisters—with long grey beards duly growing on their chins, and belike one of them duly holding in her hand a pilot's thumb. It is because Corot had no reverence for Shakespeare's text—because he was able to create in his own way, with scarcely a thought of Shakespeare, an independent masterpiece—that this picture is worthy of its theme. The largeness of the landscape in proportion to the figures seems to show us the tragedy in its essential relation to the universe. We see the heath lying under infinity, under true sky and winds. No hint of the theatre is there. All is as the poet may have conceived it in his soul. And for us Corot's brush-work fills the place of Shakespeare's music. Time has tessellated the surface of the canvas; but beauty, intangible and immortal, dwells in its depths safely—dwells there even as it dwells in the works of Shakespeare, though the folios be foxed and seared.

The longer we gaze, the more surely does the picture illude us and enthral us, steeping us in that tragedy of 'the fruitless crown and barren sceptre.' We forget all else, watching the unkind witches as they await him whom they shall undo, driving him to deeds he dreams not of, and beguiling him, at length, to his doom. Against 'the set of sun' they stand forth, while he who shall be king hereafter, with the comrade whom he shall murder, rides down to them, guileless of aught that shall be. Privy to his fate, we experience a strange compassion. Anon the fateful colloquy will begin. 'All hail, Macbeth' the unearthly voices will be crying across the heath. Can nothing be done? Can we stand quietly here while... Nay, hush! We are powerless. These witches, if we tried to thwart them, would swiftly blast us. There are things with which no mortal must meddle. There are things which no mortal must behold. Come away!

So, casting one last backward look across the heath, we, under cover of the rock, steal fearfully away across the parquet floor of the gallery.

'CARLOTTA GRISI'
A COLOURED PRINT

It is not among the cardboard glades of the King's Theatre, nor, indeed, behind any footlights, but in a real and twilit garden that Grisi, gimp-waisted sylphid, here skips for posterity. To her right, the roses on the trellis are not paper roses—one guesses them quite fragrant. And that is a real lake in the distance; and those delicate pale trees around it, they too are quite real. Yes! surely this is the garden of Grisi's villa at Uxbridge; and her guests, quoting Lord Byron's 'al fresco, nothing more delicious,' have tempted her to a daring by-show of her genius. To her left there is a stone cross, which has been draped by one of the guests with a scarf bearing the legend GISELLE. It is Sunday evening, I fancy, after dinner. Cannot one see the guests, a group entranced by its privilege—the ladies with bandeaux and with little shawls to ward the dew from their shoulders; the gentlemen, D'Orsayesque all, forgetting to puff the cigars which the ladies, 'this once,' have suffered them to light? One sees them there; but they are only transparent phantoms between us and Grisi, not interrupting our vision. As she dances—the peerless Grisi!—one fancies that she is looking through them at us, looking across the ages to us who stand looking back at her. Her smile is but the formal Cupid's-bow of the ballerina; but I think there is a clairvoyance of posterity in the large eyes, and, in the pose, a self-consciousness subtler than merely that of one who, dancing, leads all men by the heart-strings. A something is there which is almost shyness. Clearly, she knows it to be thus that she will be remembered; feels this to be the moment of her immortality. Her form is all but in profile, swaying far forward, but her face is full-turned to us. Her arms float upon the air. Below the stark ruff of muslin about her waist, her legs are as a tilted pair of compasses; one point in the air, the other impinging the ground. One tiptoe poised ever so lightly upon the earth, as though the muslin wings at her shoulders were not quite strong enough to bear her up into the sky! So she remains, hovering betwixt two elements; a creature exquisitely ambiguous, being neither aerial nor of the earth. She knows that she is mortal, yet is conscious of apotheosis. She knows that she, though herself must perish, is imperishable; for she sees us, her posterity, gazing fondly back at her. She is touched. And we, a little envious of those who did once see Grisi plain, always shall find solace in this pretty picture of her; holding it to be, for all the artificiality of its convention, as much more real as it is prettier than the stringent ballet-girls of Degas.

'HO-TEI'
A COLOURED DRAWING BY HOKUSAI

What monster have we here? Who is he that sprawls thus, ventrirotund, against the huge oozing wine-skin? Wide his nose, narrowly-slit his eyes, and with little teeth he smiles at us through a beard of bright russet—a beard soft as the russet coat of a squirrel, and sprouting in several tiers according to the several chins that ascend behind it from his chest. Nude he is but for a few dark twists of drapery. One dimpled foot is tucked under him, the other cocked before him. With a bifurcated fist (such is his hand) he pillows the bald dome of his head. He seems to be very happy, sprawling here in the twilight. The wine oozes from the wine-skin; but he, replete, takes no heed of it. On the ground before him are a few almond-blossoms, blown there by the wind. He is snuffing their fragrance, I think.

Who is he? 'Ho-Tei,' you tell me; 'god of increase, god of the corn-fields and rice-fields, patron of all little children in Japan—a blend of Dionysus and Santa Claus.' So? Then his look belies him. He is far too fat to care for humanity, too gross to be divine. I suspect he is but some self-centred sage, whom Hokusai beheld with his own eyes in a devious corner of Yedo. A hermit he is, surely; one not more affable than Diogenes, yet wiser than he, being at peace with himself and finding (as it were) the honest man without emerging from his own tub; a complacent Diogenes; a Diogenes who has put on flesh. Looking at him, one is reminded of that over-swollen monster gourd which to young Nevil Beauchamp and his Marquise, as they saw it from their river-boat, 'hanging heavily down the bank on one greenish yellow cheek, in prolonged contemplation of its image in the mirror below,' so sinisterly recalled Monsieur le Marquis. But to us this 'self-adored, gross bald Cupid' has no such symbolism, and we revel as whole-heartedly as he in his monstrous contours. 'I am very beautiful,' he seems to murmur. And we endorse the boast. At the same time, we transfer to Hokusai the credit which this glutton takes all to himself. It is Hokusai who made him, delineating his paunch in that one soft summary curve, and echoing it in the curve of the wine-skin that swells around him. Himself, as a living man, were too loathsome for words; but here, thanks to Hokusai, he is not less admirable than Pheidias' Hermes, or the Discobolus himself. Yes! Swathed in his abominable surplusage of bulk, he is as fair as any statue of astricted god or athlete that would suffer not by incarnation...

Presently, we forget again that he is unreal. He seems alive to us, and somehow he is still beautiful. 'It is a beauty,' like that of Mona Lisa, 'wrought out from within upon the flesh, the' adipose 'deposit, little cell by cell, of strange thoughts and fantastic reveries and exquisite passions.' It is the beauty of real fatness—that fatness which comes from within, and reacts on the soul that made it, until soul and body are one deep harmony of fat; that fatness which gave us the geniality of Silenus, of the late Major O'Gorman; which soothes all nerves in its owner, and creates the earthy, truistic wisdom of Sancho Pauza, of Francisque Sarcey; which makes a man selfish, because there is so much of him, and venerable because he seems to be a knoll of the very globe we live on, and lazy inasmuch as the form of government under which he lives is an absolute gastrocracy—the belly tyrannising over the members whom it used to serve, and wielding its power as unscrupulously as none but a promoted slave could.

Such is the true fatness. It is not to be confounded with mere stoutness. Contrast with this Japanese sage that orgulous hidalgo who, in black velvet, defies modern Prussia from one of Velasquez's canvases in Berlin. Huge is that other, and gross; and, so puffed his cheeks are that the light, cast up from below, strives vainly to creep over them to his eyes, like a tourist vainly striving to creep over a boulder on a mountainside. Yet is he not of the hierarchy of true fatness. He bears his bulk proudly, and would sit well any charger that were strong enough to bear him, and, if such a steed were not in stables, would walk the distance swingingly. He is a man of action, a fighter, an insolent dominator of men and women. In fact, he is merely a stout man—uniform with Porthos, and Arthur Orton, and Sir John Falstaff; spiced, like them, with charlatanism and braggadocio, and not the less a fine fellow for that. Indeed, such bulk as his and theirs is in the same kind as that bulk which, lesser in degree, is indispensable to greatness in practical affairs. No man, as Prince Bismarck declared, is to be trusted in state-craft until he can show a stomach. A lack of stomach betokens lack of mental solidity, of humanity, of capacity for going through with things; and these three qualities are essential to statesmanship. Poets and philosophers can afford to be thin—cannot, indeed, afford to be otherwise; inasmuch as poetry and philosophy thrive but in the clouds aloft, and a stomach ballasts you to earth. Such ballast the statesman must have. Thin statesmen may destroy, but construct they cannot; have achieved chaos, but cosmos never.

But why prate history, why evoke phantoms of the past, when we can gaze on this exquisitely concrete thing—this glad and simple creature of Hokusai? Let us emulate his calm, enjoy his enjoyment as he sprawls before us—pinguis, iners, placidus—in the pale twilight. Let us not seek to identify him as god or mortal, nor guess his character from his form. Rather, let us take him as he is; for all time the perfect type of fatness.

Lovely and excessive monster! Monster immensurable! What belt could inclip you? What blade were long enough to prick the heart of you?

'THE VISIT'
A PAINTING BY GEORGE MORLAND, IN THE HERTFORD HOUSE COLLECTION

Never, I suppose, was a painter less maladif in his work than Morland, that lover of simple and sun-bright English scenes. Probably, this picture of his is all cheerful in intention. Yet the effect of it is saddening.

Superficially, the scene is cheerful enough. Our first impression is of a happy English home, of childish high-spirits and pretty manners. We note how genial a lady is the visitor, and how eager the children are to please. One of them trips respectfully forward—a wave of yellow curls fresh and crisp from the brush, a rustle of white muslin fresh and crisp from the wash. She is supported on one side by her grown-up sister, on the other by her little brother, who displays the nectarine already given to him by the kind lady. Splendid in far-reaching furbelows, that kind lady holds out both her hands, beaming encouragement. On her ample lap is a little open basket with other ripe nectarines in it—one for every child.

Modest, demure, the girl trips forward as though she were dancing a quadrille. In the garden, just beyond the threshold, stand two smaller sisters, shyly awaiting their turn. They, too, are in their Sunday-best, and on the tiptoe of excitement—infant coryphe'es, in whom, as they stand at the wings, stage-fright is overborne by the desire to be seen and approved. I fancy they are rehearsing under their breath the 'Yes, ma' am,' and the 'No, ma'am,' and the 'I thank you, ma'am, very much,' which their grown-up sister has been drilling into them during the hurried toilet they have just been put through in honour of this sudden call.

How anxious their mother is during the ceremony of introduction! How keenly, as she sits there, she keeps her eyes fixed on the visitor's face! Maternal anxiety, in that gaze, seems to be intensified by social humility. For this is no ordinary visitor. It is some great lady of the county, very rich, of high fashion, come from a great mansion in a great park, bringing fruit from one of her own many hot-houses. That she has come at all is an act of no slight condescension, and the mother feels it. Even so did homely Mrs. Fairchild look up to Lady Noble. Indeed, I suspect that this visitor is Lady Noble herself, and that the Fairchilds themselves are neighbours of this family. These children have been coached to say 'Yes, my lady,' and 'No, my lady,' and 'I thank you, my lady, very much'; and their mother has already been hoping that Mrs. Fairchild will haply pass through the lane and see the emblazoned yellow chariot at the wicket. But just now she is all maternal— 'These be my jewels.' See with what pride she fingers the sampler embroidered by one of her girls, knowing well that 'spoilt' Miss Augusta

Noble could not do such embroidery to save her life—that life which, through her Promethean naughtiness in playing with fire, she was so soon to lose.

Other exemplary samplers hang on the wall yonder. On the mantelshelf stands a slate, with an ink-pot and a row of tattered books, and other tokens of industry. The schoolroom, beyond a doubt. Lady Noble has expressed a wish to see the children here, in their own haunt, and her hostess has led the way hither, somewhat flustered, gasping many apologies for the plainness of the apartment. A plain apartment it is: dark, bare-boarded, dingy-walled. And not merely a material gloom pervades it. There is a spiritual gloom, also—the subtly oppressive atmosphere of a room where life has not been lived happily.

Though these children are cheerful now, it is borne in on us by the atmosphere (as preserved for us by Morland's master-hand) that their life is a life of appalling dismalness. Even if we had nothing else to go on, this evidence of our senses were enough. But we have other things to go on. We know well the way in which children of this period were brought up. We remember the life of 'The Fairchild Family,' those putative neighbours of this family—in any case, its obvious contemporaries; and we know that the life of those hapless little prigs was typical of child-life in the dawn of the nineteenth century. Depend on it, this family (whatever its name may be: the Thompsons, I conjecture) is no exception to the dismal rule. In this schoolroom, every day is a day of oppression, of forced endeavour to reach an impossible standard of piety and good conduct—a day of tears and texts, of texts quoted and tears shed, incessantly, from morning unto evening prayers. After morning prayers (read by Papa), breakfast. The bread-and-butter of which, for the children, this meal consists, must be eaten (slowly) in a silence by them unbroken except with prompt answers to such scriptural questions as their parents (who have ham-and-eggs) may, now and again, address to them. After breakfast, the Catechism (heard by Mamma). After the Catechism, a hymn to be learnt. After the repetition of this hymn, arithmetic, caligraphy, the use of the globes. At noon, a decorous walk with Papa, who for their benefit discourses on the General Depravity of Mankind in all Countries after the Fall, occasionally pausing by the way to point for them some moral of Nature. After a silent dinner, the little girls sew, under the supervision of Mamma, or of the grown-up sister, or of both these authorities, till the hour in which (if they have sewn well) they reap permission to play (quietly) with their doll. A silent supper, after which they work samplers. Another hymn to be learnt and repeated. Evening prayers. Bedtime: 'Good-night, dear Papa; good-night, dear Mamma.'

Such, depend on it, is the Thompsons' curriculum. What a painful sequence of pictures a genre-painter might have made of it! Let us be thankful that we see the Thompsons only in this brief interlude of their life, tearless and unpinafored, in this hour of strange excitement, glorying in that Sunday-best which on Sundays is to them but a symbol of intenser gloom.

But their very joy is in itself tragic. It reveals to us, in a flash, the tragedy of their whole existence. That so much joy should result from mere suspension of the usual re'gime, the sight of Lady Noble, the anticipation of a nectarine! For us there is no comfort in the knowledge that their present degree of joy is proportionate to their usual degree of gloom, that for them the Law of Compensation drops into the scale of these few moments an exact counter-weight of joy to the misery accumulated in the scale of all their other moments. We, who do not live their life, who regard Lady Noble as a mere Hecuba, and who would accept one of her nectarines only in sheer politeness, cannot rejoice with them that do rejoice thus, can but pity them for all that has led up to their joy. We may reflect that the harsh system on which they are reared will enable them to enjoy life with infinite gusto when they are grown up, and that it is, therefore, a better system than the indulgent modern one. We may reflect, further, that it produces a finer type of man or woman, less selfish, better-mannered, more capable and useful. The pretty grown-up daughter here, leading her little sister by the hand, so gracious and modest in her mien, so sunny and affectionate, so obviously wholesome and high-principled—is she not a walking testimonial to the system? Yet to us the system is not the less repulsive in itself. Its results may be what you please, but its practice were impossible. We are too tender, too sentimental. We have not the nerve to do our duty to children, nor can we bear to think of any one else doing it. To children we can do nothing but 'spoil' them, nothing but bless their hearts and coddle their souls, taking no thought for their future welfare. And we are justified, maybe, in our flight to this opposite extreme. Nobody can read one line ahead in the book of fate. No child is guaranteed to become an adult. Any child may die to-morrow. How much greater for us the sting of its death if its life shall not have been made as pleasant as possible! What if its short life shall have been made as unpleasant as possible? Conceive the remorse of Mrs. Thompson here if one of her children were to die untimely—if one of them were stricken down now, before her eyes, by this surfeit of too sudden joy!

However, we do not fancy that Mrs. Thompson is going to be thus afflicted. We believe that there is a saving antidote in the cup of her children's joy. There is something, we feel, that even now prevents them from utter ecstasy. Some shadow, even now, hovers over them. What is it? It is not the mere atmosphere of the room, so oppressive to us. It is something more definite than that, and even more sinister. It looms aloft, monstrously, like one of those grotesque actual shadows which a candle may cast athwart walls and ceiling. Whose shadow is it? we wonder, and, wondering, become sure that it is Mr. Thompson's—Papa's.

The papa of Georgian children! We know him well, that awfully massive and mysterious personage, who seemed ever to his offspring so remote when they were in his presence, so frighteningly near when they were out of it. In Mrs. Turner's Cautionary Stories in Verse he occurs again and again. Mr. Fairchild was a perfect type of him. Mr. Bennet, when the Misses Lizzie, Jane and Lydia were in pinafores, must have been another perfect type: we can reconstruct him as he was then from the many fragments of his awfulness which still clung to him when the girls had grown up. John Ruskin's father, too, if we read between the lines of Praeterita, seems to have had much of the authentic monster about him. He, however, is disqualified as a type by the fact that he was 'an entirely honest merchant.' For one of the most salient peculiarities in the true Georgian Papa was his having apparently no occupation whatever—his being simply and solely a Papa. Even in social life he bore no part: we never hear of him calling on a neighbour or being called on. Even in his own household he was seldom visible. Except at their meals, and when he took them for their walk, and when they were sent to him to be reprimanded, his children never beheld him in the flesh. Mamma, poor lady, careful of many other things, superintended her children unremittingly, to keep them in the thorny way they should go. Hers the burden and heat of every day, hers to double the roles of Martha and Cornelia, that her husband might be left ever calmly aloof in that darkened room, the Study. There, in a high armchair, with one stout calf crossed over the other, immobile throughout the long hours sate he, propping a marble brow on a dexter finger of the same material. On the table beside him was a vase of flowers, daily replenished by the children, and a closed volume. It is remarkable that in none of the many woodcuts in which he has been handed down to us do we see him reading; he is always meditating on something he has just read. Occasionally, he is fingering a portfolio of engravings, or leaning aside to examine severely a globe of the world. That is the nearest he ever gets to physical activity. In him we see the static embodiment of perfect wisdom and perfect righteousness. We take him at his own valuation, humbly. Yet we have a queer instinct that there was a time when he did not diffuse all this cold radiance of good example. Something tells us that he has been a sinner in his day—a rattler of the ivories at Almack's, and an ogler of wenches in the gardens of Vauxhall, a sanguine backer of the Negro against the Suffolk Bantam, and a devil of a fellow at boxing the watch and wrenching the knockers when Bow Bells were chiming the small hours. Nor do we feel that he is a penitent. He is too Olympian for that. He has merely put these things behind him—has calmly, as a matter of business, transferred his account from the worldly bank to the heavenly. He has seen fit to become 'Papa.' As such, strong in the consciousness of his own perfection, he has acquired, gradually, quasi-divine powers over his children. Himself invisible, we know that he can always see them. Himself remote, we know that he is always with them, and that always they feel his presence. He prevents them in all their ways. The Mormon Eye is not more direly inevitable than he. Whenever they offend in word or deed, he knows telepathically, and fixes their punishment, long before they are arraigned at his judgment-seat.

At this moment, as at all others, Mr. Thompson has his inevitable eye on his children, and they know that it is on them. He is well enough pleased with them at this moment. But alas! we feel that ere the sun sets they will have incurred his wrath. Presently Lady Noble will have finished her genial inspection, and have sailed back, under convoy of the mother and the grown-up daughter, to the parlour, there to partake of that special dish of tea which is even now being brewed for her. When the children are left alone, their pent excitement will overflow and wash them into disgrace. Belike, they will quarrel over the nectarines. There will be bitter words, and a pinch, and a scratch, and a blow, screams, a scrimmage. The rout will be heard afar in the parlour. The grown-up sister will hasten back and be beheld suddenly, a quelling figure, on the threshold: 'For shame, Clara! Mary, I wonder at you! Henry, how dare you, sir? Silence, Ethel! Papa shall hear of this.' Flushed and rumpled, the guilty four will hang their heads, cowed by authority and by it perversely reconciled one with another. Authority will bid them go upstairs 'this instant,' there to shed their finery and resume the drab garb of every day. From the bedroom-windows they will see Lady Noble step into her yellow chariot and drive away. Envy—an inarticulate, impotent envy—will possess their hearts: why cannot they be rich, and grown-up, and bowed to by every one? When the chariot is out of sight, envy will be superseded by the play-instinct. Silently, in their hearts, the children will play at being Lady Noble.... Mamma's voice will be heard on the stairs, rasping them back to the realities. Sullenly they will go down to the schoolroom, and resume their tasks. But they will not be able to concentrate their unsettled minds. The girls will make false stitches in the pillow-slips which they had been hemming so neatly when the yellow chariot drove up to the front-door; and Master Harry will be merely dazed by that page of the Delectus which he had almost got by heart. Their discontent will be inspissated by the knowledge that they are now worse-off than ever—are in dire disgrace, and that even now the grown-up sister is 'telling Papa' (who knows already, and has but awaited the formal complaint). Presently the grown-up sister will come into the schoolroom, looking very grave: 'Children, Papa has something to say to you.' In the Study, to which, quaking, they will proceed, an endless sermon awaits them. The sin of Covetousness will be expatiated on, and the sins of Discord and Hatred, and the eternal torment in store for every child who is guilty of them. All four culprits will be in tears soon after the exordium. Before the peroration (a graphic description of the Lake of Fire) they will have become hysterical.

They will be sent supperless to bed. On the morrow they will have to learn and repeat the chapter about Cain and Abel. A week, at least, will have elapsed before they are out of disgrace. Such are the inevitable consequences of joy in a joyless life. It were well for these children had 'The Visit' never been paid.

Morland, I suppose, discerned naught of all this tragedy in his picture. To him, probably, the thing was an untainted idyll, was but one of those placid homely scenes which he loved as dearly as could none but the brawler and vagabond that he was. And yet... and yet... perhaps he did intend something of what we discern here. He may have been thinking, bitterly, of his own childhood, and of the home he ran away from.

'YET AGAIN'

SOME CRITICISMS OF THE FIRST EDITION

Mr. Edmund Gosse, in THE WORLD: 'We may find it hard to realise that Max may become a classic, but I see no other essayist who seems to have more chance of it.... There is no question of "reserved places" on Parnassus, but it is my individual conviction that where La Bruye're and Addison and Stevenson are, there Max will be.... It is perhaps his final charm as an essayist that, underneath a ceremonious style, an exquisite demeanour and advance, a low voice, a graceful hearing, a polished cadence, there exists a powerful, sometimes what almost seems a furious independence of character.'

THE TIMES: 'So few men can trifle without being silly or be intimate without being tiresome, so few have either the mental power or the unity of vision necessary for a decent transition from mood to mood, that essayists fit to be ranked with Steele, Addison, Stevenson, are still few. Mr. Max Beerbohm has proved his title.... There, where every idea is the author's, and every phrase is scrupulously adapted to the best expression by the author of his own idea, we get the true originality in art. Through all the play of fancy, the wit and humour, the swift transitions, the caprice and jesting, that ultimate sincerity shines; and it is that which lights Mr. Beerbohm's fine taste and knowledge of his craft to beauty.'

THE DAILY TELEGRAPH: 'As an artist whose medium is the essay, Mr. Max Beerbohm should stand for this generation as Lamb stands for the first generation of the nineteenth century.'

THE DAILY NEWS: 'He has wit, and charm, and good humour—and these are the qualities which characterise this completely delightful volume of essays.'

THE MORNING LEADER: 'Max sees himself in a hundred different ways. In any capacity he is unique. He remains our best essayist.'

THE OBSERVER: 'Charles Lamb a' la Max is never obtrusive. It is only the ghost of him that stalks in and about. We soon fall away from the reminiscence; and the caricaturist becomes a personality.'

Mr. Sidney Dark in THE DAILY EXPRESS: 'Max is always delightful in his dainty, leisurely tolerance of everybody and everything. No other living writer could have produced "Yet Again." It is individual—and thoroughly good to read.'

THE EVENING STANDARD: 'Mr. Beerbohm is always in holiday mood; and this we gradually catch from him. We begin by enjoying him; we end by enjoying life and ourselves.'

THE NATION: 'Blessed are they who possess the gift of extracting sunbeams from cucumbers.... The simplicity of Mr. Beerbohm's themes serves but to enhance the elegance of his mind.'

Mr. G. S. Street in THE ENGLISHWOMAN: 'I trust sincerely I shall not damage his reputation if I say that the play of his fancy is never inconsistent with two strong qualities of his mind and temperament, a sound judgment and a kindly heart.'

Mr. W. H. Chesson in THE DAILY CHRONICLE: 'He is undoubtedly one of our benefactors. He excels in the humour which creates humour.'

THE GLOBE: 'In their different ways, all these essays will delight the appreciative reader, and we can only bid him or her buy, beg, borrow, or steal Max's latest volume immediately.'

Mr. James Douglas in LONDON OPINION: 'The style of these essays is not eccentric, and yet it is dyed with the hues of a personality as rich and rare as Elia's own, There is no contemporary prose which is so uncorrupted by current influences, and which is so sure to defy the corrosion of time. In a hundred years it will not be a dated or derelict thing. Its colour and its cadence will delight the connoisseur then as the colour and cadence of Lamb's prose delights him now.'

THE MORNING POST: 'He is naturally gifted with something that is called talent in life and genius after death.'